DOCTOR WHO
AND THE CARNIVAL
OF MONSTERS

Based on the BBC television serial *The Carnival of Monsters* by Robert Holmes by arrangement with the British Broadcasting Corporation

TERRANCE DICKS

Number 8 in the Doctor Who Library

A TARGET BOOK
published by
the Paperback Division of
W. H. ALLEN & Co. PLC

A Target Book
Published in 1977
by the Paperback Division of
W. H. Allen & Co. PLC
44 Hill Street, London W1X 8LB

Reprinted 1979
Reprinted 1980
Reprinted 1982
Reprinted 1984
Reprinted 1985

Printed and bound in Great Britain by
Anchor Brendon Ltd, Tiptree, Essex

ISBN 0 426 11025 0

Contents

I

Dangerous Arrivals

With a strange groaning sound, the blue police box appeared from nowhere. A very small, very pretty fair-haired girl came out, and looked cautiously around. She was in a dimly-lit, metal-walled enclosure, and the air was full of strange smells ...

A tall white-haired man, elegant in velvet smoking jacket and ruffled shirt, followed her out of the police box locking the door behind him. 'I tell you there's no need to be suspicious, Jo. I've been here before and the air's perfectly ...' he sniffed, '... fresh!' he concluded, on a rather less certain note.

Jo Grant looked indignantly at the Doctor. Really she'd only herself to blame. After the terrifying adventure of the Three Doctors,* the Time Lords, the Doctor's mysterious and all-powerful superiors, had rewarded him by restoring his ability to travel in Time and space in the TARDIS. As eager as a child with a new toy, the Doctor had persuaded Jo to accompany him on what he called 'a little test flight' to a very attractive-sounding planet named Metebelis Three.

Jo looked around her. 'Lakes like blue sapphires, he says,' she muttered. 'Jewelled deserts and mountains of blue crystal, he says ...' She turned back to the Doctor. 'It's hot, it's dark and it *smells!*'

The Doctor sniffed. No doubt about it, she was

* See 'Doctor Who—The Three Doctors'

right. 'That's very odd ...'

'Sort of *farmy*,' added Jo.

The Doctor sniffed again, and subjected the evidence of his nose to a rapid analysis. 'Nothing to worry about. Gaseous sulphides in a fairly low concentration.' He rubbed his chin. 'Very odd, that, Jo. I assure you, the last time I was here, the air was like wine.'

Jo gave him another look. 'Doctor, are you sure we're where you think we are? Can you really drive the TARDIS properly without the Time Lords helping you?'

'My dear Jo,' said the Doctor huffily. 'I don't *drive* the TARDIS, I programme it. And, according to programme, this is Metebelis Three, famous blue planet of the Acteon galaxy.'

Before Jo could reply, she became aware of a steady thump, thump, thump, filling the air around them. 'We're in some kind of a machine,' she said. 'And it's moving!'

'You're right. Well, come on.'

Jo hung back. 'Where are we going?'

'To find out where we are.'

'I thought you knew that?'

'Well, I do. I just want to convince you, that's all!'

They picked their way through the semi-darkness, which seemed to be filled with mysteriously-shaped lumpy objects, most of them with sharp edges. There was a sudden flurry ahead, and Jo clutched the Doctor's arm. 'Something moved!'

The sounds died down and they pressed cautiously on. They came to a wooden pen, with feathered shapes clucking inside. Jo laughed. 'Look—it's chickens!'

Solemnly the Doctor bowed before the cage. 'Greetings! We come as friends.'

'Doctor, what are you doing?'

'When you've travelled as much as I have, Jo, you'll learn not to jump to conclusions. These *look* like chickens, but they could be the dominant life-forms on this planet.' The Doctor leaned over the pen. 'Greetings,' he said again. There was no reply.

'Try clucking,' suggested Jo. Before he could reply she went on, 'Doctor, those things not only look like chickens, they *are* chickens. And what about this?'

She pointed to the side of a near-by crate. The Doctor looked. Despite the gloom it was possible to make out the stencilled capital letters. They read, 'SINGAPORE'.

'The Acteon Galaxy, you said?'

Taken aback, but not yet defeated, the Doctor looked round. Near by, a ladder led up into the darkness above them. 'Come on, Jo,' he said, and started to climb.

Shaking her head at his obstinacy, Jo followed, pausing only to say a quick 'Good-bye!' at the chickens. They clucked back at her.

At the top of the ladder was a hatch. The Doctor lifted it. Behind him on the ladder Jo peered through the gap. She saw decking, a rail, more cargo-hatches—and an Indian seaman in shabby overalls walking past. 'Metebelis be blowed,' she whispered. 'This is just an ordinary old cargo-ship, Doctor. You've landed us back on Earth.'

As the terrifying adventure which followed was to prove, Jo had never been more wrong in her life.

Meanwhile, more arrivals were taking place ...

9

The Spaceport of Capital City, on the planet called Inter Minor, was baking in the heat of the planet's twin suns. It was a busy colourful scene as the massive cargo-rockets loaded and unloaded in their separate bays. Ground cars and cargo-trains scurried to and fro like ants at the feet of the towering metal mountains of the great space-rockets. Cursing and sweating, the Functionaries worked steadily away, loading and unloading the cargo.

Capital City was in the middle of a boom. By decree of President Zarb, the planet's new ruler, Inter Minor had emerged from its long self-imposed seclusion, and was busily trading with the other planets in its galaxy. Many years ago, the planet had been ravaged by Space Plague, brought in by a traveller from some foreign planet. In a hysterical over-reaction, the Inter Minorans had cut themselves off completely from *all* other planets, forbidding both travel and commerce. After years of bitter political struggle, the new progressive party, led by President Zarb, had come to power, and Inter Minor had opened up its frontiers.

President Zarb hoped by this measure to relieve some of the pressures on Minoran society. His other plans included a gradual improvement in the lot of the Functionaries. This meant persuading the Official caste to give up some of their many privileges—an undertaking which was provoking bitter resistance.

The strangest thing of all about this strange world of Inter Minor was the fact that its people had been divided for so long into two different social classes that they had gradually evolved into two different species.

The largest class was that of the Functionaries. They were short and stocky with coarse, lumpy, unfinished features. They looked as if they'd been slapped together out of rough clay, by a rather poor sculptor. They wore rough serviceable clothing in heavy-duty plastic. Their purpose, their *function* was to work. Work, food and sleep, that was a Functionary's life. For generations they had accepted this fate uncomplainingly. But now things were beginning to change ...

Then there was the ruling caste—the Officials. They were mostly tall and thin, grey-faced and grey-robed. Grey-minded too, for the main part. The Officials' code insisted on rigid formality with all display of emotion totally suppressed. They were the Officials, rulers by right and custom. Not all, of course, had utterly closed minds. President Zarb and his supporters were aware of the necessity for change. But the bulk of the Officials were set in their old ways. They had accepted Zarb only because they hoped he would save them from revolution.

A thunderous rumble shook the Spaceport as yet another cargo-rocket descended slowly on to its pad. As soon as touchdown was complete, a cargo-shute was connected to its main hatch, and an assortment of goods began tumbling down, to be seized by waiting Functionaries, hurled on to cargo-trains and driven from the Spaceport.

From a viewing ramp, two Officials watched the process with gloomy disdain. Their names were Kalik and Orum. Kalik's bored manner concealed fierce intelligence and burning ambition, while Orum's masked only complacent foolishness. Kalik was small and wiry, while Orum had a tendency to plumpness.

It was Kalik who spoke first. 'The cargo-rocket we

were ordered to meet has arrived.' Like all Officials, he had no inhibitions about stating the obvious.

Orum nodded gravely. 'One must prepare oneself to go and encounter these—aliens.' The last word came out as a hiss of distaste.

Kalik sighed. 'Reluctantly, one agrees.'

The two grey figures began descending the ramp into the teeming confusion of the Spaceport.

Meanwhile, something very strange was happening at the unloading rocket. On the cargo-shute had appeared two unmistakably humanoid figures. Arms and legs waving wildly they tumbled down the shute with the other containers. At the bottom they scrambled to their feet, waving away the Functionaries, who looked quite capable of loading them on to a cargo-train without a second glance.

First to reach the ground was a middle-aged, middle-sized humanoid clad in tattered golden finery. Boots, tunic, tights and cloak had all once been magnificent, but like their wearer had seen better days. The humanoid, by race a Lurman, by name, Vorg, dusted himself down, gazing around him with keen alert eyes under fierce bushy eyebrows, and stroking an equally bushy moustache.

Beside him a moment later landed Shirna, an attractive young female Lurman. Her clothes too were ornate but worn, and the many neat darns and patches showed a desperate attempt to keep up appearances.

Shirna hit the ground in a flaming temper. Never a girl to hide her feelings she lost no time in letting Vorg know it.

'Top of the bill, he says!' she cried dramatically, looking round at the hot and dusty Spaceport. 'Treated like a star, he says!'

Shirna drew a deep breath. She had plenty more to say. Before she could get into her stride Vorg yelled, 'Oh no, the Scope!' A gaudily decorated cylindrical object was tumbling down the chute with the other cargo. Vorg pushed aside a Functionary, caught hold of the Scope and started lowering it gently to the ground. 'Come on, Shirna, help me,' he yelled. 'This thing's our living, remember.'

Between them they managed to wrestle the Scope off the chute and over to a small alcove under one of the ramps. The Scope was a tallish, fattish cylinder just under the size of a man. On top was an elaborate control-panel, inset with rows of lights and switches. Viewing apertures were inset at eye-level all round. There was a maintenance and service panel low on one side. Flashy colours and elaborate ornamentation gave the Scope the look of something between a jukebox and a 'What The Butler Saw' machine. And indeed, the Scope was a kind of peepshow—though of a very elaborate and unusual kind.

Like its owners, the Scope had an air of seedy magnificence about it. It was a technological wonder that had come down in the world. Vorg was checking it over—it was a temperamental machine and the journey might have upset it—when Shirna jabbed an elbow in his ribs. 'Look out—here they come!'

Vorg looked. Two grey-robed figures were threading their way through the crowd towards them. Vorg saw how deferentially the brawny Functionaries moved aside for them. Immediately he assumed the humble and ingratiating smile that was his inevitable response to any kind of authority.

13

Vorg's preliminary encounter with Minoran official-dom was to be temporarily delayed. A disturbance had broken out in the next cargo-bay. One of the Functionaries had stopped work and had climbed up on to a ramp. This in itself was a serious offence. The raised ramps leading to the upper City were only for the use of Officials. Worse still, the Functionary was daring to make some kind of speech, distracting his fellows from their work. As if fascinated by his audacity, more and more Functionaries were drifting away from their work to swell the gathering crowd beneath the ramp.

Vorg and Shirna could understand nothing of the Functionary's guttural speech, but judging from the growls of agreement the crowd was on his side. Shirna glanced at the two near-by Officials to see how they were taking all this. To her horror, she saw that one of them had produced a blaster from beneath his robes . . .

Kalik levelled the blaster and fired. The rebellious Functionary swayed, slumped and crashed down on to the crowd. They all drew back, terrified. A squad of uniformed Functionaries, under the command of a Military Official, pushed their way to the body and dragged it off. The Functionaries returned to their work. The little rebellion died away without trace, like the ripples from a stone thrown into a pond.

Orum gave a satisfied nod. It pleased his sense of fitness to see order restored. Casually he asked, 'You eradicated him?'

Kalik put his blaster away. 'No, no. Merely rendered him unconscious. Our Medical colleagues have asked that all such specimens be taken alive.'

'He *will* be disposed of?' asked Orum worriedly.

'Naturally. But first his mental and nervous system will be analysed. Our colleagues wish to discover if some disease or mutation is causing these outbreaks of rebellion.'

It did not occur to Kalik that it was not the rebellious Functionaries who were abnormal, but the conditions under which they had to live and work.

His conscience clear and untroubled, he put away his blaster.

'Now one must deal with these aliens.'

Terrified by this display of casual ruthlessness, Vorg and Shirna quailed as the two Officials bore down upon them.

2

The Monster from the Sea

Peering through the partly-open hatch, the Doctor looked at the peaceful maritime scene around him. Everything suggested that Jo was perfectly right. They were on a small cargo vessel, probably in tropical waters. And yet ...

'Appearances can be deceptive, Jo,' he warned. 'I still feel there's something very wrong here.'

The small figure on the ladder below him gave an impatient snort. 'Something wrong with the way you steer the TARDIS, more like it. We *are* still on Earth, aren't we?'

The Doctor shook his head decisively. 'No, that's impossible. We don't seem to be on Metebelis Three, but we're not on Earth either.'

'Never admit you're wrong, do you?' hissed Jo.

The Doctor grinned. 'That's impossible, too. The sailor's gone now. Let's take a look around.'

Blinking in the hot sunlight, they climbed out of the hatch, lowered it quietly behind them. They moved across the deck of the little ship to the super-structure, and stepped through a doorway. Now they were in a short metal-walled passage. From an open door at the other end they heard voices. 'Splendid dinner this,' someone was saying in fruity English tones. 'Absolutely topping.'

Jo and the Doctor crept along the passage and

peeped through the half-open door. They saw a small but well-furnished saloon. Three people were sitting around the table over the remains of a meal. An attractive young girl was pouring herself a cup of coffee and a rosy-faced, white-haired man in a rather rumpled tropical suit was pouring himself a large whisky from a decanter. A handsome young man in the uniform of a ship's officer was listening politely to the older man, but giving his real attention to the girl.

The older man, whose name was Major Daly, took an appreciative sip of his whisky. 'You say the cook's a Madrassi, Andrews?'

'I believe so, sir.' Lieutenant Andrews somehow managed to give a polite reply to this question without taking his eyes from the girl. Clare Daly, the Major's daughter, smiled, well aware of the young officer's interest.

Daly nodded thoughtfully. 'Find the Madrassi boys a bit idle, meself. Won't have one on the plantation. Still, I must say your fellow knows how to curry a chicken.' Daly nodded towards the decanter. 'Sundowner, old chap?'

Andrews shook his head. He glanced appealingly at Clare Daly who smiled and took mercy on him. Finishing her coffee she said demurely, 'Lieutenant Andrews and I thought we'd take a turn around the deck. Care to join us, Daddy? It's a glorious evening.' Clare knew she was on safe ground. It was highly unlikely that her father would forsake his armchair and his book—to say nothing of the whisky decanter.

Sure enough, Daly grunted and shook his head. 'No, you and young Andrews don't need me. You run along. I'm going to do a spot of reading. Determined to finish this book before we reach Bombay.'

Clare laughed. 'We're due tomorrow, remember. How much have you got left?'

'Only another two chapters.'

Andrews stood up. 'We'll see you later then, sir. Come along, Clare—twenty times round the deck is a mile!'

The Doctor and Jo saw him usher the girl through a second door at the far end of the saloon. They watched Major Daly settle himself into a comfortable armchair, his book on his lap. He read only a page or two before his head started nodding. The book slipped from his lap and he began to snore.

The Doctor gave Jo a nod and they slipped into the saloon. They crept up to Daly who slept on happily. Then they heard approaching voices. Andrews and Clare were walking along the deck, just outside the window.

'I love musical comedies,' Clare was saying. 'I saw "Lady Be Good" four times. And wasn't that young American fellow marvellous? Fred something-or-other ...'

Her voice died away. Jo and the Doctor stood up. Now the only sound breaking the silence was that of Daly's contented snores.

The Doctor looked round the little saloon, shaking his head unbelievingly. 'In spite of everything, Jo, I still say this isn't Earth.'

'All right, Doctor, I'll convince you.' Jo picked up Daly's book and turned to the title page. 'Look—date of publication, nineteen twenty-six.'

The Doctor took the book, looked at it, and shook his head. 'I know, Jo. Every little detail, but ...'

Jo was hopping up and down with frustration. 'You're so *stubborn*, Doctor. You ought to have an L-plate on that Police Box!'

The Doctor said quietly. 'Come on, Jo, we're going back to the TARDIS. I don't know what's happening here, but I don't like it ...' He moved towards the door, but stopped when Jo didn't follow. 'What's the matter? Do you want to stay here?'

'I just want you to admit the truth, Doctor. Instead of swanning round in some distant galaxy, we've slipped back fifty years in time. We're on a little cargo boat in the Indian Ocean and ...'

Jo's tirade was cut short by a shattering roar from outside the cabin. They heard a scream from Clare, a sudden shout from Andrews. Daly started to mutter and stir, and the Doctor pulled Jo quickly into the corridor, just as Clare and Lieutenant Andrews came running back. Daly stumbled to his feet. 'What's going on?'

Andrews led Clare across to her father. 'Some kind of sea monster, sir. It's hideous.'

There was another roar, and a jolting crash shook the ship as something huge slammed against it.

The Doctor led Jo to a porthole and they looked out. An enormous sea-creature was swimming around the boat, its savage head waving about on the end of a fantastically long neck.

The monster roared once again, then plunged back into the sea. They saw it swimming away for a while, then it disappeared beneath the waves.

'What was that thing?' Jo gasped.

'A plesiosaurus,' said the Doctor. 'And if this is

nineteen twenty-six—the plesiosaurus has been extinct for millions of years!'

In the saloon, Daly was staring fascinatedly out of the porthole. 'I say, it's gone back into the sea.'

'I'll get a rifle,' said Andrews. 'Just in case it decides to come back again. Look after Clare, will you, sir?'

'Of course, my boy. Come along, m'dear.' The Major led the shivering Clare to a comfortable chair and settled her down. He looked almost yearningly out of the porthole. 'By Jove, what a monstrous beast!'

Clare buried her face in her hands. 'It was awful, horrible,' she sobbed.

'There, there, child,' said her father soothingly. 'We'll take a shot at it, if it does come back. What a head, eh? Love to have that on the Club wall!' He went on staring out of the porthole.

Jo and the Doctor were now on the far side of the saloon door—they had to pass it to get back to their cargo-hatch. They tiptoed past it very quietly. Unfortunately, Clare Daly happened to look up exactly as they were framed in the open doorway. She stared at them in amazement, and let out a little cry. Daly turned and came over to the door. 'Hullo!' he said wonderingly.

'Hullo!' said the Doctor cheerily. 'Topping day, what?'

'I say, just a minute old chap,' said Daly. 'Are you two passengers?'

'Only temporarily.' The Doctor made an attempt to get away, but by now Daly had come into the corridor and was blocking their exit. He stared at them. 'Temporarily?'

Jo decided to take a hand. 'Uncle means just until we reach Bombay,' she said brightly.

Clare had come over to join her father. 'I thought *we* were the only passengers,' she said. 'Where did you come aboard?'

'Oh—er Port Said,' said Jo hurriedly, hoping her geography was accurate.

Clare looked puzzled. 'I still don't understand why we haven't met before.'

Jo felt she was getting in deeper and deeper. And the Doctor wasn't any help. He just smiled blandly and let her flounder on.

'Well, my uncle here hasn't been well,' she said, getting a bit of her own back. 'We've mostly stayed below.'

Daly looked at the Doctor sympathetically. 'Poor traveller, eh? Not used to it, I suppose?'

The Doctor rose to this immediately. 'On the contrary sir, I happen to be a very experienced——'

Andrews came in, a rifle in his hand. He stopped at the sight of the little group, then crossed the saloon to them. 'Who are these people?'

Daly stared at him. 'Don't *you* know, Andrews? They said they got on at Port Said.'

Andrews shook his head. 'Stowaways, eh? Where have you been hiding yourselves?'

Jo drew a deep breath, and then gave up. She looked at the Doctor. 'You tell them—uncle.'

To Vorg and Shirna's surprise, the two Minoran officials didn't approach them at once. They stopped a little way off and stood quietly talking, glancing occasionally at the two Lurmans. They seemed to be working out something. Meanwhile, a crowd of Functionaries was gathering around the alcove, staring curiously at the two aliens and their strange machine.

Vorg, busily checking over the machine, didn't notice them at first, Shirna jabbed him in the ribs again. 'Hey, Vorg!'

He looked up and she indicated the crowd of curious faces. Vorg smiled. Crowds were his business. 'Well, well, well, we seem to be getting an audience. I'd better start the pitch.'

'What here?'

'Why not? A real showman can work anywhere.' Vorg raised his voice to a practiced carrying chant. 'Roll up, roll up, me lucky lads.'

The Functionaries crowded closer.

'Hang on a minute,' said Shirna. Hurriedly she brushed down her costume, and struck a dramatic pose gesturing towards the Scope.

Vorg went into his patter. 'Roll up, roll up, and see the real live monster show. A whole Carnival of Monsters, live and clawing in this amazing device. See them living wild in their natural habitat! A miracle of inter-galactic technology! Roll up, roll up ...'

The two Minoran officials watched these goings on from a safe distance. 'So—those two strange beings are Lurmans,' said Kalik distastefully.

Orum consulted a document. 'It appears that the male is called Vorg, and the female Shirna.'

'Ridiculous, these alien names. One is relieved that their physical form is familiar. One feared they might have four heads. Though it is still unpleasant to have to fraternise with any alien race.' Despite the fact that he was the President's brother, Kalik was one of the old school.

'Nevertheless, Commissioner Kalik, one has one's duty to perform,' Orum said solemnly.

'One will wait for Commissioner Pletrac. He is the Chairman of our little tribunal. Let him perform *his* duty. Meanwhile, one will observe these aliens a little longer.'

Vorg wasn't enjoying his usual success with his showman's patter. In fact it seemed rather to alarm the Functionaries. Slowly they began drifting away from the alcove. Shirna, who had been watching his efforts with cynical resignation, glanced towards the Scope. A light was flickering on the control panel. She attracted Vorg's attention with her usual jab in the ribs.

Vorg abandoned his patter and went over to the Scope. 'It's nothing,' he said uneasily. He thumped the side of the Scope with his fist. The light still flickered. 'I'm sure it's nothing.'

'That light indicates a systems defect, doesn't it?'

'No, no. Just a loose connection. Nothing of consequence.'

'A systems defect,' said Shirna firmly.

Vorg gave the Scope an angry kick. 'Of all the times to go wrong!' He took off his coat and rolled up his sleeves. 'I'll have to take off the inspection plate. Get the tools will you, Shirna?'

Shirna began passing him tools from a well-worn bag. While Vorg wrestled with the inspection panel she looked at the Minoran officials. 'Not very friendly, are they?'

Vorg grunted. 'They're Officials. Officials are never friendly.'

A third Minoran Official had arrived to join the other two. He to was grey-robed and grey-faced, but his white hair and stooped shoulders gave him an air of age and rank. Pletrac was still very spry, despite his years. He bustled up to Kalik and Orum. 'One hears that yet another Functionary has gone berserk,' he said in shocked tones.

'One witnessed the event,' said Kalik coldly. 'In fact, one dealt with it.'

Orum shook his head sadly, 'One cannot understand why they do it.'

'But then, one is not a Functionary,' said Kalik in a bored tone.

Plectrac looked sharply at him. 'It is a growing problem. As members of the Official caste, we must all share President Zarb's concern.'

'Functionaries have no sense of responsibility,' said Orum sadly. 'Give them a hygiene chamber and they only store their issue of fossil fuel in it.'

In his alcove, Vorg had finally managed to get the inspection panel off the Scope. 'Pass the micro-scanner,' he ordered. Shirna fished a telescope-like device from the bag and handed it to him.

Vorg peered through it, jiggled it about, then gave a sudden grunt of satisfaction.

Shirna leaned over his shoulder. 'Have you located the fault?'

'There's a bit of foreign matter inside circuit three.'

'Can you get it out?'

'I think so. It's really only a matter of unscrewing the circuit baseplate. Have a look for the micro-driver, will you?'

As Shirna searched in the untidy jumble of the tool-bag, Vorg peered again through the micro-scanner. 'It's a funny thing,' he said thoughtfully. 'This foreign body—it seems to be a kind of blue box!'

3

The Giant Hand

The Doctor's attempts at explaining their presence on
board had met with little success. Reluctant as always
to disclose the existence of the TARDIS, he had spun
a long and complicated story about having to leave
Port Said because of some urgent secret mission which
he wasn't free to disclose. The Doctor thought it quite
a good story—but unfortunately Lieutenant Andrews
didn't believe a word of it. 'I suppose you realise the
Captain could have you put in irons,' he said grimly.

'My dear fellow, do you really think that's necessary?'

'Not if you start telling me the truth.'

Clare Daly was beginning to feel sorry for the two
newcomers. 'Oh do stop bullying them, John,' she
said.

'That's right, stop bullying us,' said Jo, grateful for
the unexpected ally.

Major Daly too seemed to think things were going
a bit far. 'I say, why don't we all have a drink and talk
this over like civilised people?'

'An excellent idea,' said the Doctor promptly. 'I'll
have a small——'

'Major Daly!' cut in Andrews firmly. 'These people
are certainly stowaways and quite possibly criminals.'

'Oh dash it all,' protested Daly. 'The fellow *is* a
Sahib, you know.'

'Nevertheless, this is *not* a social occasion.'

'Still don't see why we shouldn't offer basic hospitality ...'

Andrews smiled grimly. 'I'd like to offer them the hospitality of your cabin, sir. There's a good strong lock on the door. They can wait there till the Captain's free to see them.'

'Oh very well,' said Daly. 'Put 'em in my cabin by all means.'

Andrews gestured sharply with his rifle. 'Right, you two. This way.'

As he marched them off down the corridor, the Doctor said, 'You see? We should have left when I wanted to.'

'Well, who got us here in the first place?' hissed Jo.

Andrews marched them along to a cabin door and opened it. Just outside the door was an octagonal metal plate set into the floor. The Doctor looked at Andrews. 'Are there many of these on the ship?'

'Many of what?'

'*These* things,' said the Doctor, pointing. 'Are there others, or is this the only one?'

Andrews stared at him. 'There's nothing there.'

Jo looked down at the plate and then up at Andrews. 'You mean you can't see it?'

Andrews raised the rifle. 'Get in that cabin!' he ordered sharply. They went in.

Major Daly's cabin was small but comfortable with the usual brass and mahogany ship's furnishings. Bunk, wash-stand, writing desk, armchair, clothes locker. Everything seemed utterly normal.

Andrews stood in the doorway. 'I don't know what you two are up to. But I've a crew of lascars who try

27

to make a fool of me every trip. They haven't succeeded yet, and neither will you!'

Jo gave a cheeky grin. 'Don't underestimate us!'

The Doctor was studying a framed plan of the ship on the cabin wall. He read the lettering underneath. 'I say, old chap, is this ship the S.S. *Bernice*?'

'Are you trying to pretend you didn't even know that?'

'I didn't. Now I do, and it makes everything much clearer. Thank you.'

Andrews felt he was being made fun of, and he didn't care for it. 'All right! I'm going to lock you in here till the Captain is ready to see you. He's a very busy man, so that might not be for a long time.'

Andrews left, slamming the door hard behind him. They heard the key turn in the lock and his footsteps going away. Jo turned to the Doctor. 'All right. You said everything was much clearer. Explain!'

'Well, relatively speaking. An octagonal plate in the floor, and a prehistoric monster in the sea. Yes, it's really most interesting.'

The Doctor stretched out comfortably on the bunk. Jo sank into the chair. 'Do you really think Andrews couldn't see that metal plate?'

'I'm sure he couldn't, Jo. It was blocked from his consciousness. You see, it isn't really part of the fabric of the ship.'

'Not part of the ship? A great lump of . . .'

The Doctor smiled infuriatingly. 'Exactly. A lump of what? Not steel, iron, copper, aluminium. That metal isn't known on Earth.'

Jo waved a hand round the little cabin. 'We *must* be on Earth. This cabin, the ship, the chickens, the

28

people ... You're not going to tell me Major Daly's an alien from another planet?'

The Doctor pointed to a calendar beside the bunk. 'Look at this. Daly's been keeping track of the date.' Jo saw that the calendar was for the year ninteen twenty-six. It was open at the month of June, and someone had crossed off the days as far as June the fourth. The Doctor nodded to the wall plan. 'And what about the name of the ship? Doesn't that mean anything to you?'

'No! should it?'

'For a time the S.S. *Bernice* was the centre of a mystery as famous as that of the *Marie Celeste*.'

Jo was alarmed. 'What happened?'

'Nobody ever knew,' said the Doctor mysteriously. 'A freak wave was the favourite explanation—but the Indian Ocean was as calm as a mill pond that night.'

'You mean the ship *sank*?'

'She *vanished*, Jo. Two days from Bombay, on the night of June the fourth, the *Bernice* disappeared from the face of the Earth—or rather the sea.'

Jo looked at the calendar. 'June the fourth? But that's today!'

'Intriguing, isn't it?' said the Doctor cheerfully.

Jo was looking at the cabin clock. 'Shall I tell you something else intriguing? When we came in here that clock said twenty-five to eight. Now look at it!'

The Doctor looked. The clock's hands were at twenty to six. 'So you've noticed that? Well I've noticed something else. It's still broad daylight outside.'

'So?'

'If it really is after dinner, and if we really are in

29

the Indian Ocean—it should be pitch dark by now.'
The Doctor swung his long legs from the bunk and
made for the door, rattling the handle experimentally.

'Sonic screwdriver?' suggested Jo.

The Doctor looked a little sheepish. 'I'm afraid
that only works on electronic locks, Jo. This is a
simpler lock and we need a simpler tool.'

Jo produced a bunch of skeleton keys. 'Like this?'

The Doctor stared at her. 'Why on earth are you
carrying those things around with you?'

'If I've learned one thing in travelling about with
you, Doctor, it's that sooner or later we're bound to
get locked up! Allow me!' Watched by the astonished
Doctor, Jo started to pick the lock.

It didn't take her long to get it open, and they went
out into the corridor. Jo thought they'd make straight
for the TARDIS, but the Doctor knelt by the metal
plate in the floor and started to examine it. 'Works by
anti-magnetic cohesion,' he muttered.

'Can you open it?'

'Not without a magnetic core-extractor.'

'That's that, then,' said Jo, relieved. 'Let's get back
to the TARDIS.' Their positions had become reversed.
Jo was anxious to get away, while the Doctor wanted
to stay and investigate further.

'As a matter of fact,' said the Doctor slowly. 'I do
happen to have a magnetic core-extractor somewhere
in the TARDIS.'

Jo sighed. 'Of course. I might have known you
wouldn't travel without one!'

The problem about getting back to the TARDIS
was that it involved going past the passenger saloon.
They crept towards it, and as they approached the

open door, they heard voices.

'Splendid dinner, this,' someone was saying in fruity English tones. 'Absolutely topping. You say the cook's a Madrassi, Andrews?'

They heard Andrews' polite reply. 'I believe so, sir.'

'Find the Madrassi boys a bit idle, meself. Won't have one on the plantation. Still, I must say your fellow knows how to curry a chicken. Sundowner, old chap?'

Then came Clare's voice. 'Lieutenant Andrews and I thought we'd take a turn round the deck. Care to join us, Daddy? It's a glorious evening.'

'No, you and young Andrews don't need me. You run along. I'm going to do a spot of reading. Determined to finish this book before we reach Bombay.'

Astonished, Jo heard the whole sequence of events replay itself exactly as before. They heard the clink of the decanter as Daly settled himself in the armchair. Clare and Andrews went out on to the deck, talking just as before.

Jo pulled the Doctor's sleeve. 'Come on, Doctor, let's get out of here.'

The Doctor didn't move. 'Hang on a moment, Jo. I've got a theory about what's happening here ... and we should get confirmation any minute.'

'*Nothing's* happening here,' said Jo. 'That's what's so creepy. They're just going round and round like a stuck gramophone record!'

'That's right. They've been programmed to repeat a simple behaviour pattern.'

'That monster, the plesiosaurus. Has that been programmed too?'

'I imagine so.'

31

'But there weren't any plesiosauruses in nineteen twenty-six!'

'Exactly. I'm afraid that, historically speaking, this collection is a bit of a jumble.'

Jo shook her head. 'Are you trying to tell me that this ship, and everyone on it, are all part of some kind of collection?' She looked around. 'Everything seems so ordinary.'

'Jo, have you ever seen a child at the seaside, filling a bucket with sea creatures? After a while they behave quite normally. Only the boy looking down at them knows their environment has changed.'

'Human beings are rather more intelligent than whelks!'

'And these specimens were collected by more sophisticated methods than a net and pail. But the principle's the same.'

'I'm sorry, Doctor, I just don't believe it.'

There came a shattering roar from outside the ship. They heard a scream from Clare, a sudden shout from Andrews. Daly stumbled to his feet. 'What's going on?'

The Doctor pulled Jo back around a corner as Andrews and Clare rushed past them. They heard his voice from the saloon. 'Some kind of sea monster, sir. It's hideous.' There was another roar and a jolting crash as something enormous slammed against the ship. The Doctor led Jo to the porthole, and they saw the many-fanged head on the incredibly long neck as the plesiosaurus swam round the boat.

They ducked quickly back into hiding as Andrews's voice came from the saloon.

'I'll get a rifle, just in case it decides to come back

again. Look after Clare, will you, sir?'

Andrews rushed out of the saloon and disappeared on deck.

'Now,' said the Doctor. 'Quick, before she looks up!'

With Clare's head still buried in her hands, and Daly staring out of the window, they ran past the open door of the saloon. As they passed it, Daly's voice floated out. 'What a head, eh? Love to have that on the Club wall ...'

Keeping low, the Doctor and Jo scurried along the deck. In the bows, Andrews, rifle in hand, a few terrified lascars beside him, was staring after the plesiosaurus as it sank roaring back into the sea. The Doctor lifted the cargo-hatch and they both descended into a hot darkness that smelled of chickens ...

The familiar shape of the TARDIS stood in the corner and they made their way through the gloom towards it. Jo hoped they'd be able to go inside and take off—but she should have known better.

'Hang on here a moment,' said the Doctor reaching for his key. 'I'll pop inside and get the magnetic core-extractor.'

'Can't we just go home Doctor?'

The Doctor's voice came through the open door of the TARDIS. 'Where's your scientific curiosity, Jo? Don't you want to know what's going on?'

'Not much, no.'

The Doctor came out of the TARDIS, an oddly-shaped gadget in his hand, and locked the door behind him. 'Just a quick look at what's behind that metal plate, and we'll be off I promise ...'

There came a sudden terrified scream from Jo and

the Doctor swung round. Jo pointed upwards, too frightened to speak.

A section of the cargo-hold high above them had just opened out, as if on some kind of hinge. Through the gap an enormous hand had appeared ... the hand of a giant. It groped around vaguely for a moment, then started descending towards them ...

4

Trapped!

Jo and the Doctor cowered away, crouched behind a pile of crates as the giant hand seemed to reach down for them. It came lower ... lower ... then, with a slight change of direction its index finger and thumb closed on the TARDIS. It lifted the police box as a man might pick up a box of matches from a drawer. Holding the TARDIS, the giant hand disappeared through the gap.

The Doctor yelled, 'Hey, that's mine. Bring it back!' His only answer was an echoing clang as the section of hold swung back and darkness returned.

Jo's face popped up from behind a crate. 'Doctor, that hand ... has it gone?'

'It has. And it's taken the TARDIS with it.'

Jo stared upwards. 'But there's no way through. Are you sure?'

'Part of the hold swung open.'

Jo looked at the steel wall. 'But that must weigh tons and tons.'

'You saw the size of that hand.'

'But we've been up there,' persisted Jo. 'There's only the deck.'

'There must be an optical illusion as well as a temporal one. I told you this was no ordinary ship.'

'And now we're trapped on it—with the TARDIS gone ...'

'Don't worry,' said the Doctor reassuringly, 'It's only a matter of finding where it's gone and getting it back!'

Jo was almost speechless. 'Only? Well, where do we start?'

'We start by finding a way off this ship.' The Doctor started towards the ladder. Wondering just how they were going to get off a ship in the middle of the ocean, Jo followed him.

Vorg withdrew his hand from the Scope with a satisfied grunt. 'Got it!'

Shirna leaned over his shoulder. 'Let's have a look.'

Vorg kept his hand inside the Scope's inspection hatch. 'Got to keep it within the miniaturisation field. Here it is.'

Shirna looked at the little blue box. 'That was causing all the trouble?'

'Apparently. Must be electrically charged in some way.'

'How did it get in there?'

'Search me. Maybe it was in there all along and just got displaced. Anyway, I'll put it here on the spare-parts shelf.'

Vorg straightened up and started to replace the hatch. 'Just in time,' whispered Shirna. 'Our grey friends are coming over at last.'

Their long deliberations finished, the three Minoran Officials were striding towards them. Pletrac in the lead, as befitted his rank, Kalik and Orum flanking him. The Minorans paused at a safe distance, unwilling to risk alien contamination.

'One must now collect their data-strips,' said Pletrac. 'Orum?'

Orum stepped back, shuddering. 'Physical contact?' he asked in a horrified tone.

'You are Chairman,' said Kalik in his waspish tone. 'One suggests you approach them, Pletrac.'

The old man settled his robes on his shoulder. 'One has no fears,' he said rather nervously. 'Your Lurman is a simple fellow. Good natured and trusting, he responds well to firm leadership, and is capable of great loyalty.'

'Perhaps we should import them to replace our Functionaries,' sneered Kalik.

Pletrac strode up to Vorg and Shirna. 'We friends,' he said, in a rather quavering voice.

Vorg produced his lowest bow. 'Your worship!' Shirna curtsied prettily. There was an embarrassed pause.

'Er—you give magic talk boxes,' said Pletrac.

Vorg and Shirna stared at each other. Vorg whispered, 'I think he wants our data-strips.'

Shirna fished out two plastic micro-strips and held them out to Pletrac. 'It's all right,' she said encouragingly. 'We don't bite!'

The old man snatched the strips and scuttled back to his fellows. There were more deliberations.

Shirna shook her head. 'They're a weird lot. I don't know why you were so keen to come here, Vorg.'

Vorg leaned forward confidentially. 'This planet cut itself off from the rest of the galaxy after the great Space Plague. They've only just opened their frontiers again. Traders are coming in—but we're the first entertainers! No one else saw the opportunity!'

'You mean none of them will have seen anything like the Scope before?'

'Exactly. Think of it, Shirna. That great audience out there, a whole world of them. We'll go back to Lurma with a million credit-bars.'

Pletrac and his tribunal were studying the data-strips on a portable computer terminal. Pletrac looked up. 'These seem to be in order.'

'The record is incomplete,' objected Kalik. 'There is no reference to the machine.'

'Machines are harmless,' said Pletrac querulously. 'We have examined the data-strips and found them in order. What more should we do?'

'Examine the machine,' snapped Kalik. He shot a glance at Orum.

'One agrees,' said Orum hurriedly. 'It would be advisable.'

Pletrac moved over to Vorg and Shirna. Kalik and Orum followed him. Pletrac handed back the data-strips. 'These are in order. But the tribunal requires to know the purpose of your machine.'

Vorg was shocked. His moustache and eyebrows seemed to bristle with outrage. 'Machine, your worships? The Scope is no mere machine!'

Kalik was unimpressed. 'Then what is it?'

Vorg cleared his throat impressively. 'The Scope is a unique artistic achievement. The supreme creative invention of our age! It is my proud privilege to bring its many wonders to your noble planet. You will be amazed, you will be astounded——'

Kalik's dry voice cut across the flow of Vorg's oratory. 'Is it a machine within the normal meaning of the word?'

Vorg heaved a dramatic sigh. 'Machine is such a paltry description, your worship.'

'Cease prevaricating,' snapped Kalik. 'What is the machine's function. What does it *do*?'

Vorg sighed. Some people had no poetry in their souls. 'Well, your worships,' he began. 'It's like this ...'

Since the octangonal metal plate was just outside Major Daly's cabin, the Doctor and Jo followed the same route as before. They were working their way along the deck towards the passenger saloon, slipping from cover to cover, when they heard voices coming towards them. They had just time to duck behind a lifeboat as Lieutenant Andrews and Clare came along the deck, still discussing musical comedies. 'I absolutely adored Chu Chin Chow,' Clare was saying. 'Daddy took me when I was a little girl.'

Andrews laughed. 'I tell you the whole thing's absolute rubbish. I've sailed into Shanghai fifty times, my girl, and I know what Johnny Chinaman's really like!'

They passed on their way chatting happily. Jo whispered, 'I suppose we're due for the monster bit again any time now?'

'Very probably,' said the Doctor.

Sure enough there came the shattering roar, and a savage head on a long waving neck appeared out of the sea. 'Let's not see it round again,' said Jo. 'When you've seen one plesiosaurus, you've seen 'em all.'

There were the same roars from the monster, the same shouts of alarm from Andrews and Clare. Andrews hurried Clare back to her father, and ran off to the arms locker.

'Come on,' said the Doctor, 'now's our chance.'
They ran through the door, along the passage and tiptoed towards the open door to the passenger saloon.
As they reached it Clare was in her chair, face in
hands, and Daly was gazing out of the porthole.

'What a head, eh?' he was saying. 'Love to have
that on the Club wall!' But this time he turned a frac-
tion earlier—and caught sight of Jo and the Doctor
creeping past. Obviously it was possible for minor
variations to occur within the programmed pattern of
events. Major Daly gaped at them. 'Hullo,' he said.

'Topping day, what?' said the Doctor.

'Absolutely splendid,' replied Daly politely.

The Doctor struggled to remember his early twen-
tieth-century slang. 'Well, twenty-three skidoo, must
get on, eh? Pip, pip!'

Daly came to the saloon door. 'I say, are you passengers?'

'Don't you remember,' said Jo. 'You asked us that
before?'

Daly looked at her in disbelief. 'How could I? I've
never bally well seen you before in my life.'

The three Minoran Officials listened to Vorg's explanations in sceptical silence. Pletrac attempted a
summing-up. 'If I understand you so far, it appears
that you travel from planet to planet with this—
machine performing some kind of ritual? For what
purpose?'

Shirna decided to take a hand. 'We're *entertainers*.'
she explained patiently.

'Entertainers?' Pletrac was none the wiser. 'Explain the term.'

'We put on a show,' said Shirna. 'You understand?' She did a little tap-dance by way of demonstration.

The three Minorans recoiled in alarm. 'No,' said Pletrac.

'Our purpose is to *amuse*,' confirmed Vorg. 'Nothing serious, nothing political ...'

Kalik frowned. 'Amusement is prohibited. It is purposeless.'

Pletrac led his two colleagues to one side. 'President Zarb has lifted that restriction. His thinking is that lack of amusement is causing these outbreaks of rebellion among the Functionaries.'

'More anti-productive legislation,' hissed Kalik.

Orum shook his head mournfully. 'One wonders where it will end.'

'One can see where it will end, Orum. The Functionaries will take over.' Kalik spoke dryly.

Pletrac looked sharply at him. 'It is not the Functionaries who dream of power, Kalik. Since President Zarb is your brother, one hoped for more loyalty.'

'One simply speaks one's thoughts,' said Kalik smoothly.

The old man glared at him. 'Your thoughts are as plain as your ambitions.'

'How dare you!'

Orum tried to smooth over the quarrel. 'Pletrac, Kalik, please. We are here simply to decide whether to grant these entertainers an entrance visa.'

Kalik spoke first. 'In view of their subversive purpose and their dubious machine, one moves that the application be rejected.'

41

'Motion opposed,' said Pletrac.

Kalik looked at Orum, who said hurriedly. 'Motion supported.'

Pletrac sighed. 'Very well.' He led the little group back to Vorg and Shirna. 'I regret to tell you that your application for a visa has been rejected by this Tribunal. You will be allotted space on the next outbound cargo-thruster.'

Vorg was shattered at the sudden dissolution of his dreams of wealth. 'But, your worship,' he stammered. 'Please, I beg of you. We spent our last credit-bar on the journey here.'

Kalik gave him an indifferent look. 'That was unwise,' he said turning away.

Vorg made a final effort. 'If your worships would permit me to demonstrate the wonders of the Scope, I'm sure you would be ready to reconsider. The Scope is not only amusing but educational too!'

Pletrac was old-fashioned and conservative, but he was also fair minded. He hadn't cared for the way in which Kalik had forced through the Tribunal's decision. 'The suggestion is reasonable,' he said firmly. 'Demonstrate!'

Vorg bustled around overjoyed. 'If your worships would take up their positions at the viewing apertures. This way, your worships.'

He arranged the three Minoran Officials at viewing apertures around the Scope, and moved to the controls. 'Now, if you will gaze deeply into the glo-sphere ...'

The viewing apparatus of the Scope produced a mild hypnotic effect, making the viewer feel part of the scene he was witnessing. Immediately the three Minorans seemed to have left the familiar bustle of the

Spaceport, and to be standing on some bleak, alien planet. Towards them lumbered a huge ape-like creature dressed in rough leather clothing. Pletrac jumped back in alarm—and was relieved to find himself still in the Spaceport. 'What was that thing?'

'A primitive life-form called the Ogron,' said Vorg. 'I believe they are used as servants by some race called Daleks. If your worship will return to the viewing-place?' Vorg twiddled controls.

The Minorans were transported to a steaming tropical swamp.

'With a bit of luck,' said Vorg. 'I shall be able to show you the pride of my collection—the Drashigs.' Far away in the swamp there was a roar and a splash. Then nothing more.

'Amazing,' said Kalik ironically.

Vorg was apologetic. 'The Drashigs have no intelligence centres, unfortunately, so it's impossible to control them. I'll switch over to the Terrans. Less spectacular, but extremely controllable! One of their planet's native sea-monsters has been added to their habitat for increased variety! You should see them react when it appears.'

This time the Minorans found themselves in a kind of living-chamber, in which a number of Terrans were talking agitatedly.

'The species was discovered in a distant galaxy,' said Vorg in his best lecturer's voice. 'You will note the strong resemblance these little chaps bear to our own life-form.'

Kalik shuddered. 'The resemblance is unpleasant. Are they going to *do* anything?'

43

Vorg felt his show was failing to impress, and decided to give it a boost. 'Observe closely, your worships. By a simple adjustment of the aggrometer—so —these peaceful Terrans can be made to behave in an amusingly aggressive manner.'

In the passenger saloon of the S.S. *Bernice*, the programmed sequence of events was playing itself out. One again the Doctor and Jo had become part of it. Just as before they had tried to elude Daly and Clare, just as before Andrews had turned up, this time with a couple of armed seamen, and disbelieved their explanations. It looked as if they were to be locked up in Daly's cabin all over again.

A low humming note rang through the ship. No one except Jo and the Doctor seemed to notice it. But suddenly the atmosphere became hostile and threatening.

His eyes blazing with anger Andrews shouted, 'So you persist in sticking to this ridiculous story, do you?'

The Doctor said sharply, 'And what if I do, sir?'

Andrews tossed his rifle to a sailor, stripped off his coat and started to roll up his sleeves. 'Then I propose to thrash you within an inch of your life!'

The three Minorans stared fascinatedly into the Scope.

'What ritual are they performing now?' asked Orum.

Vorg looked into his viewing aperture. 'Two of the males are about to engage in physical combat, your worship.'

Jo Grant felt she was in some kind of nightmare. Lieutenant Andrews was rolling up his sleeves over brawny arms. The Doctor too had taken off his coat, and was rolling up the sleeves of his ruffled shirt.

Jo looked at Andrews, so much younger and stronger than his opponent. 'Doctor, you can't,' she whispered.

The Doctor seemed caught up in the prevailing madness. 'I most certainly can,' he said briskly. 'It will give me the greatest of pleasure to teach this insolent young puppy a much needed lesson.' Tone and manner were quite unlike his normal self.

Jo turned to Major Daly and Clare. Surely they would make some protest. 'Please,' she pleaded, 'you've got to stop them. It isn't fair.'

Neither father nor daughter seemed to hear her. They were leaning forward excitedly, eyes shining with bloodthirsty eagerness, waiting for the fight to begin.

Preparations completed, fists clenched and raised, the two opponents moved towards each other . . .

5

Inside the Machine

Jo didn't know much about boxing, but she couldn't help noticing the differences in styles. Andrews moved forwards in a crouch, shoulders hunched, chin tucked in, fists weaving protectively in front of him. He spoke through gritted teeth. 'I think I ought to warn you, I used to box for my school.'

The Doctor's stance was straight-backed and upright, right hand protecting his chin, left arm stretched out full-length. He moved with brisk skipping steps. 'And I should warn *you*, I used to spar with John L. Sullivan!'

The fight was short and savage. The two men came together in a flurry of blows. Jo saw the Doctor dodge and block Andrews's punches with careless ease. The Doctor's long left arm shot out and his fist caught Andrews on the cheekbone, then again on the nose. Stung by the two painful blows Andrews swung a wild right uppercut at the Doctor's chin. The Doctor dodged it with ease and sunk a savage right hook into the younger man's solar plexus.

Air whooshed from Andrews's body, his face went grey and he collapsed like a leaking balloon, slumping slowly to the ground.

Jo saw the Doctor's face change ... He leaned over his fallen opponent, appalled at what he had done, and was about to help him to his feet. Jo looked round.

Clare, Major Daly, the two sailors, all were staring open-mouthed at the gasping Andrews. She grabbed the Doctor's coat from a chair. 'Hurry, Doctor, this way!' The Doctor stared wildly at her. Jo grabbed him by the arm and dragged him out of the saloon.

They started to run towards Daly's cabin but another armed seaman appeared at the end of the passage. They turned and ran the opposite way, out on to the deck of the ship.

In the saloon Andrews was struggling to his feet. He grabbed his rifle and turned to the seamen. 'Get after them. Cover the aft companionway! Quick, man! Shoot on sight!' They all ran from the saloon.

Major Daly and Clare followed after them. 'Don't want to miss the fun, do we?' puffed Daly, as he hurried along.

Hidden behind a lifeboat Jo watched the Doctor get back into his coat. 'Extraordinary,' he was muttering. 'Remote control aggression-stimulation. Felt it myself, till I realised what was happening. I shouldn't have hit that poor young fellow so hard.'

There was a shout of 'There they are!' The crack of a rifle and a bullet whined close to them.

'Never mind him, Doctor,' said Jo. 'You worry about us!'

They sprinted across the decks, ducking and weaving to dodge the bullets. In the chase that followed, it seemed to Jo that they must have covered every inch of the ship. They were hunted across decks, up and down companionways, into another cargo-hold and out again. Always behind them was the sound of running feet, the voice of Andrews harrying on his lascar seamen, and the crack of rifle-fire whenever they were spotted. As they ran along a stretch of open deck, Jo gasped, 'How many times round the deck is a mile?'

'Too open here,' called the Doctor. 'Let's try that door.'

They ran to the door. The Doctor grabbed the handle, but the door was locked from inside. There was a rifle-shot and a bullet ricocheted off metal. Jo looked up. Andrews, rifle at his shoulder, was crouching on a companionway above them. The Doctor grabbed Jo's wrist and dragged her round the corner. They found another door, and luckily this one did open. Once through, the Doctor swung it closed behind them and locked it—just as bullets smacked against the other side of the steel door.

Back inside the ship they ran quickly along the narrow metal passages. 'Look,' said Jo, 'there's the dining saloon.'

'That's right! And there's the entrance to Daly's cabin, and there's that metal plate!' The Doctor quickly knelt beside the plate, taking the core-extractor from his pocket.

'How does it work?' asked Jo.

The Doctor began moving the little device along the edges of the plate. 'Simple. You hold it flat and move it along the edges of the plate—like this . . .'

'On your feet!' They looked up at the harsh command. Andrews, Daly and a handful of lascar seamen, all carrying rifles, were running along the passage. The Doctor glanced round for a weapon. There was a flare-pistol clipped to a wall rack and instinctively he reached for it—but too late. Andrews's rifle barrel jabbed his ribs.

Slowly the Doctor straightened up. Andrews slid

back the bolt on his rifle. 'We've had just about enough of your nonsense,' he said angrily. 'The punishment for piracy on the High Seas is death!' There was a fanatical gleam in his eye, and he was quite beyond the reach of reason. 'Firing party!' he shouted.

The lascar seamen shuffled themselves into a line, rifles raised to cover the Doctor and Jo. 'No!' shouted the Doctor. 'You can't ...'

'Ready, aim ...'

A low throbbing note sounded through the ship. For a moment Andrews, Daly and the others froze like statues. Then lowering his rifle, Andrews turned to the Major. 'I say, sir, I think I heard the dinner gong.'

'Splendid, hope there's something decent tonight. I'm feeling rather peckish.'

'I think you'll enjoy the curry, sir. Our cook's a Madrassi, you know. First-rate chap ...' Andrews turned to the sailors. 'Well, don't hang about, you chaps, back to your duties, chop, chop.'

The sailors hurried away, and Andrews and Daly strolled off down the corridor, chatting amiably.

Abandoned by their former pursuers, Jo and the Doctor stared at each other unbelievingly.

Vorg looked up from the controls of the Scope. 'I've turned the Aggrometer right down,' he explained. 'Can't keep it on for long or the specimens start damaging each other.' Almost disappointedly, the Minorans looked up from the Scope. They moved aside again, and began a whispered conference among themselves.

Shirna sidled up to Vorg. 'Hey, I was watching that

last bit, when they were all running round. Those two they were chasing—have you ever seen them before?'

'Really, Shirna, how do I know. They all look alike to me,' muttered Vorg irritably. He was looking at the Minorans, wondering if there was any chance of them changing their minds. No doubt about it, they'd been pretty impressed by the Scope.

'Vorg, listen! Those two Terrans are *new*!'

He stared at her. 'Nonsense. That's impossible. How could they get in there? It's a closed system.'

Shirna shrugged. 'Search me. But I tell you they're strangers.'

Vorg scratched his head. 'Well, there's only one explanation, then. They're breeding.'

'They were fully-grown specimens,' said Shirna impatiently.

Vorg sighed. Expelled from the planet, now strangers in the Scope. It just didn't seem to be his day ...

Jo watched the Doctor slide the core-extractor along the edge of the plate. 'Why did they all go rushing off like that?'

'Because the influence that was acting on them must have been turned off suddenly. Produced a temporary memory-blackout. Ah, got it.' The metal plate slid back revealing a black opening.

Jo peered down it. 'Seems to be the mouth of some kind of shaft, Doctor. Like a giant metal pipe ...'

'Right,' said the Doctor. 'Down you go, then.'

Jo slid into the dark opening. The Doctor grabbed the flare-pistol from the wall rack, stuffed it in his pocket, then followed her. The panel slid shut over their heads.

Jo found herself sliding down a long, smooth, metal tube. Luckily the pipe was tilted at an angle so the drop wasn't too steep, and she found she could slow her descent by bracing herself against the sides. Suddenly the pipe ended, and Jo shot out into space. She fell only a few feet, landing with a bump on a metal floor. A few seconds later, the Doctor landed beside her. They picked themselves up and looked around. Jo gasped in amazement. They were deep inside some enormous and incredibly complex machine.

Stretching above and below and on every side were coils, circuits, wires as thick as cables, moving wheels, pistons and cogs. Some of the machinery hummed and throbbed. Valves and circuits gave off an eerie flickering glow. Jo felt like an ant that had wandered inside the back of a television set—very small, very vulnerable and very much out of place.

She looked up at the Doctor. Hands on hips, head thrown back, he was gazing absorbedly around him. On his face was an expression of pure rapture. 'Just look at that filter circuit, Jo,' he said delightedly. 'What a beautiful piece of work. Now then—this must be the return system, so that will be the power-feed over there ... The Doctor crawled into a narrow space between two circuits, and his muffled voice echoed out. 'Yes, yes, it is! Come and look at this, Jo. Magnificent!'

Jo tugged hard on one of his projecting legs and he came reluctantly out. 'Doctor, where are we?' she demanded. 'What is this thing?'

'What is it? My dear Jo, it's a magnificent example of an early pulse mechanism based on the principle of

caeusium decay. Oh, this is absolutely vintage stuff!'
Such was his enthusiasm that he seemed to have completely forgotten all their problems.

'I take it this isn't the ship's engine room?'

'Of course it isn't, we're not even *on* the ship any longer.'

'So where's the TARDIS?'

'No idea. Probably been taken outside the machine entirely. Grit in the works, you see. We'll find it.'
Then he was off again.

'Just look at this capillary hydraulic pump. Have you ever seen anything like it?'

Jo hadn't and didn't much want to. 'Doctor, the only reason we came inside this clockwork maze was to find the TARDIS. So if the TARDIS is outside, let's start finding our way out.'

The Doctor nodded reluctantly. 'I suppose you're right, Jo. Well, we'd better begin by following this circuit.'

They set off along a narrow metal tunnel, festooned with many-coloured wires ...

After yet another mini-conference, the three Minoran officials approached Vorg and Shirna once more. Vorg gave Shirna a confident nudge. 'I knew it. My little demonstration won them over. They're going to change their minds and let us stay.'

Pletrac was leading the way, as usual. He cleared his throat and said, 'One thing still puzzles the Tribunal. How were you able to influence the actions of the specimens as you did? Surely all these pictures are recorded?'

Vorg sighed. Hadn't they understood *anything*? Patiently he explained. 'On the contrary, your worship, the Scope is good old-fashioned live entertainment. The picture on the viewing aperture glo-sphere is a projection of what is actually taking place.'

In horrified tones, Kalik hissed, 'Do you mean all those creatures are actually *living* in there?'

Vorg nodded proudly. 'That is so, your worship, all happy and content in their own miniaturised environments. The incorporation of a simple temporal loop ensures that they repeat the same basic patterns hour after hour ...'

Kalik wasn't listening. He had rounded on Pletrac in savage satisfaction. 'You see where these new policies lead, Pletrac? This machine, this Scope, contains actual live alien creatures. The Lurman has imported them without a licence.'

Pletrac flushed with rage as he turned to Vorg. 'Well? Is this true? Is it?'

Vorg was taken aback by the violence of the old man's reaction. Although he knew the Minorans' history, he hadn't realised the full extent of their hatred and fear of other life-forms. He made his deepest bow. 'Your worship, have I done something to offend?'

Kalik was whispering fiercely to Pletrac. 'Our laws expressly forbid the mass transportation of unscrutinised alien life-forms to this planet. Even my well-meaning brother Zarb has not yet repealed *that* law.'

'The creatures will have to be destroyed,' said Orum.

Vorg caught the word. 'Destroyed? My specimens?'

Pletrac nodded agitatedly. 'Destroyed—and immediately!'

'You can't do that,' pleaded Shirna. 'Our livelihood

53

depends on the Scope.'

'We are just simple strolling players, your worship,' began Vorg.

Pletrac ignored them. He drew back the sleeves of his robe to reveal a wrist-communicator. 'Send an Eradicator detachment to loading-bay two immediately.' He turned back to Vorg and spoke more gently. 'I am sorry, but the specimens and the machine must be destroyed at once. The regulations are quite clear.'

He turned away, as if fearing contamination. The three officials waited at a discreet distance.

Vorg glared after them. 'Bloodthirsty barbarians!' He sat down tiredly beside the Scope.

Shirna joined him. 'Dim-witted yokels, you said they were. Twist them round your little finger. Have them eating out of your hand. A fine mess we're in now, aren't we?'

Vorg raised his head indignantly. 'You're not blaming me, are you?'

'Yes I am,' said Shirna flatly. 'I should have stayed with the All-Star Dance Company.'

'Third-rate bunch of hoofers,' grunted Vorg scornfully.

'At least I always had a few credit-bars to my name. And we *never* travelled by cargo-thruster!'

The wrangle was interrupted by the sound of marching feet. A squad of uniformed Functionaries pushing an enormous electronic cannon were forcing their way through the crowd.

'Eradicator detachment, this way!' shouted Pletrac. The impressive, deadly-looking device was wheeled over, and its muzzle trained on the Scope.

Always the showman, Vorg jumped to his feet. He

54

stood between the Eradicator and the Scope, arms spread wide.

'Stand aside,' ordered Pletrac.

'This is murder,' shouted Vorg. 'Assassination! Massacre! I am not without influence, you know. There will be complaints!'

Pletrac coughed. 'Commence eradication,' he said quietly.

Vorg leaped clear. A uniformed Functionary bent over the Eradicator controls. There was a hum of power and the metal parts of the Scope began glowing red.

The Doctor and Jo were nearing the end of the metal tunnel when it began to vibrate. Smoke filled the air and it became appallingly hot. Jo staggered against a wall and jumped back. The metal was hot too. 'Doctor,' she gasped, 'what's ... happening ...' Overcome by the heat, she slid to the floor.

Vorg looked on glumly, as the Scope took the full blast of the Eradicator's power. 'There goes our living!'

Shirna was almost crying. 'More than our living. What about the specimens? Don't you realise—they're all being killed while we watch!'

6

The Monster in the Swamp

In theory the Scope should have disintegrated completely under the beam of the Eradicator. But it did nothing of the kind. It just sat there, glowing brightly, but still obstinately present. Smoke poured from the bearings of the Eradicator as it started to overheat.

'Cease eradication,' ordered Pletrac hurriedly. The hum of the Eradicator died down. The glow faded from the Scope. It appeared quite unharmed.

The silence was broken by Kalik. 'Bravo!' he said ironically.

'The machine must be armoured,' spluttered Pletrac. 'There must be protective forcefields ...'

'We have lost face,' said Kalik coldly. 'Our technology has proved insufficient.'

Timidly Orum said, 'The Eradicator was designed primarily for use against organic substances ...'

Pletrac looked hopefully at him. 'So the creatures inside the Scope ...?'

'Organic. The Eradicator will certainly have destroyed them.'

Pletrac gave Kalik a satisfied look. 'Good. That was our objective. The Scope in itself is unimportant. I shall report that the operation has been successful.' He strode away.

Vorg and Shirna were examining the Scope. It was

still a little warm to the touch, but that was all. 'Really built, eh?' said Vorg admiringly. 'None of your modern rubbish.'

'Are you sure it isn't damaged?' asked Shirna sceptically.

Vorg started to check the circuits.

The Doctor dragged Jo along the rest of the passage into a clearer space beyond. To his relief, the terrible vibration was dying down, and already it seemed to be getting cooler. He lowered Jo gently to the still-warm floor. After a moment she muttered and stirred. He put an arm round her shoulders. 'Come on, Jo, sit up.'

'Not yet. I'm only half-cooked.' Groggily she got to her feet. 'What happened?'

'I've no idea. We were in a bit of a hot spot for a while, weren't we?'

'It's the giants. They know we're in their machine. They're trying to kill us ...'

The Doctor thought she might well be right—but there was no point in telling her so. 'Nonsense,' he said cheerfully. 'Why should they attack us? We've done nothing to harm them.'

'Then what did happen?'

'I've no idea. One problem at a time, eh? We've still got to find our way out of here. Let's try this way! It looks very promising.'

'Promising, huh?' Jo was mopping her brow with her handkerchief, which by now was little more than a sweat-soaked rag. She tossed it aside, and followed the Doctor.

Vorg gave the controls another twiddle and peered into his viewing aperture. At once he seemed to be on a bleak moonscape. Giant silvery figures with strange projecting handles for ears were striding towards him. But everything was fuzzy and blurred. Shirna looked over his shoulder. 'That's marvellous. Who's going to pay us good credit-bars to look at a blob in a snowstorm?'

Vorg rubbed his hands. 'The heat must have affected the vision-circuit. Soon fix that. The main thing is, the specimens are all right. Those protective force-fields must be really something.'

He didn't notice the grey figures of Kalik and Orum lurking behind a pillar. They had sidled closer to eavesdrop. They slipped away again. Once they were at a safe distance, Kalik gave Orum a reproving stare. 'So the specimens were destroyed, Orum?'

'The machine must have in-built defensive force-fields, as the humans said.'

'The Scope is well defended,' said Kalik. 'It is we who have no defences. President Zarb and his council of fools have betrayed us.'

Orum glanced round. 'That is dangerous talk—even for the President's brother.'

Kalik lowered his voice. 'Zarb has cut down our defensive forces. The Eradicator is our sole protection. Now we have just demonstrated its efficiency to those two Lurman spies!'

'You really think the two Lurmans are spies?'

Kalik looked at Orum. What a gullible fool the fellow was. Of course Kalik didn't believe Vorg and Shirna were spies. Or rather he didn't much care if they were spies or not. His aim was to use their presence to embarrass Pletrac, and his brother Zarb, as much as possible. Kalik enjoyed stirring up trouble for its own sake. He was determined to lose no opportunity of making political capital out of Zarb's error in allowing the aliens and their Scope to land on the planet.

Kalik looked across at Vorg, who was fiddling about inside the Scope. 'Perhaps at this very moment he is using a transmitter, reporting all our weaknesses to his masters!' Orum looked at him wide-eyed. Summoning him with a nod to follow, Kalik drew his blaster and moved stealthily towards the Scope.

Jo had been trailing after the Doctor for what seemed a very long time, and they were no nearer reaching an exit. She suspected they were lost, though naturally the Doctor refused to admit it.

They came to the mouth of a shaft and suddenly Jo paused to pick up a crumpled scrap of cloth. 'We're going round in circles, Doctor. Look, here's the handkerchief I dropped.'

The Doctor looked at it. 'I'm afraid you're right, Jo.'

'Then we're lost,' said Jo hopelessly.

'No, of course not. Just a little mislaid. Tell you what, we'll try a new tack.' The Doctor looked round, racking his brains. Suddenly he snapped his fingers, 'Got it! You see that bulge in the wall, there? That must be part of the housing for the impeller vanes.'

Jo gave him a tearful look. 'That makes me feel much better, knowing that.'

The Doctor grinned. 'I thought it would. You see,

that means there must be an air-duct near by. And where is that air ducted from?'

'Outside?' said Jo hopefully.

'Right!'

Jo wiped the tears from her eyes. 'Sorry to be such a misery, Doctor. It's just this terrible feeling that we're not getting anywhere.'

'I know. Our trouble is we're walking about inside the blueprint instead of looking down on it——'

Jo screamed. A colossal steel spike was moving along the shaft towards them. The Doctor grabbed Jo and they flattened themselves against the wall. The shaft slid by them, probed about a little, then withdrew. Relieved, Jo watched it go. Then she screamed again. From far down the shaft an enormous eye was peering at her ...

Vorg straightened up from the Scope's service panel. He put down his screwdriver and rubbed a hand across his eyes. 'You know, Shirna, I'm not given to seeing things, but for a moment I thought there were Terrans actually in the works.'

Shirna didn't answer. Vorg glanced up to find Kalik's blaster inches from his head. 'Slowly, Vorg,' said Kalik threateningly. Vorg turned and straightened up.

Orum was holding a blaster on Shirna. 'All right,' said Orum, with quavering determination. 'Where is your transmitter?'

Vorg wondered if everybody was going mad. 'Your worship, I know nothing of any transmitter ...'

'What were you doing in there?' snapped Kalik.

'Minor adjustments. Just silly little minor adjustments.'

'There was a fault in the video circuits,' confessed Shirna eagerly.

'Nothing of consequence, your worships,' pleaded Vorg. 'Nothing at all ...'

Kalik waved his blaster. 'Orum, search that cavity.'

Orum knelt and peered dubiously inside the Scope.

Kalik said, 'If he finds a transmitter in there, Vorg ... you're dead!' Vorg groaned, and Shirna put her arm round him.

'What's all this about a transmitter, Shirna?' he whispered.

Shirna shrugged. 'Search me. I suppose he means a beam pulser. You know, for sending messages.'

'We haven't got one in the Scope, have we?'

'You ought to know. You told me you were an electronics expert.'

Vorg sighed. 'Well, not really an expert. To tell you the truth, I've never really understood these technicalities ...' He caught sight of Kalik's blaster again and shivered. 'Would your worship be kind enough to move that away. It's very frightening.'

Orum's muffled voice came from inside the Scope. 'It is rather dark in here. One can see little.'

'Search, Orum!' ordered Kalik impatiently. 'If there is a transmitter it will be disguised.'

Orum straightened up. 'There is only this.' He held a tiny blue box in his hand.

'Aha!' said Kalik, giving Vorg an accusing look. 'And what is that?'

'Mere bric-a-brac, your worship. Loose material. I found it inside the circuits some time ago. Better keep it inside the Scope or ...'

He was too late. Orum felt the box *move* in his hand and dropped it in panic. It fell to the ground, there was a fearsome groaning sound and the box *grew*, expanding rapidly to the size of a Police Box—which is what it was, at least on the outside.

Near by Functionaries fled in panic. Kalik blanched but held his ground, jabbing his blaster in Vorg's ribs. 'Bric-a-brac! All right, what is it? Let's have the truth.'

'I tell you I found it,' said Vorg desperately. 'It was causing interference.'

Orum approached the blue box cautiously. 'Perhaps it is a secret weapon. Why did it expand in size?'

'I tried to warn you,' said Vorg. 'You took it out of the Scope's compression-field. Left out too long—after a minute or two, things regain their normal size. If only you hadn't ...'

'It is an alien artefact,' said Kalik. 'How did it get in there?'

Before she could stop herself, Shirna blurted out 'The Terrans! It must have been the new Terrans, Vorg.' She looked at the Officials. 'I saw two new Terrans, strangers, in circuit three.'

Vorg managed a smile. 'Your worships, my assistant is an imaginative child ...'

'Silence!' ordered Kalik. 'Orum, is it possible for Terrans to conceal themselves in this device?'

Orum looked doubtful. 'It wouldn't be possible for our technology. Terrans may be more advanced.'

Kalik nodded. Things were building up nicely. 'The Terrans are not even from our galaxy. Who knows what new diseases they may bring with them.' Kalik knew well that rumour of a new Space Plague was a sure way to spread panic on Inter Minor. 'And if they find some exit from that machine ...'

Vorg tried to redeem the situation. 'Your worships need have no fear. Each group of specimens is enclosed in a separate living zone. The Scope is completely and utterly escape-proof!'

Jo and the Doctor had found the air-duct at last after much weary clambering over, under and between the inner workings of the Scope. Once the duct had been found they had wriggled inside it and wormed their way along its narrow length—only to find the far end blocked by a heavy metal hatch.

Jo groaned in despair. The Doctor studied the hatch thoughtfully. 'Don't worry, it's not as formidable as it looks. If I can cut through this locking-bar here ...'

'I suppose you've got a file in your pocket?'

'Well as a matter of fact ...' The Doctor fished out a length of metallic string, looped it round the bar and began sawing it to and fro. 'String file,' he explained airily. Jo smiled. No doubt the Doctor felt he'd evened things up for her skeleton keys. The Doctor sawed away patiently. Some while later, Jo leaned forward to inspect his progress.

'It's nearly through,' she said encouragingly.

The Doctor rubbed his aching wrist. 'So am I,' he groaned. The locking bar gave way at last. The Doctor moved it aside and opened the hatch. 'I think I'd better go first. We don't really know what's out there.' He climbed through the opening

'The TARDIS, I hope,' muttered Jo as she followed him. The Doctor helped her down on the other side.

Jo looked round astonished. She wasn't in a machine at all now. She was in a cave. Through its entrance she could see a steaming, swampy, featureless landscape stretching away into the distance.

Pletrac had returned to the cargo-bay and was listening to the story of recent events. He looked at the TARDIS with severe disapproval. 'We really cannot have this sort of thing. Regulations are quite clear on the subject.'

Vorg did his best to reassure him. 'I assure you, your worship, if the Scope is handled properly, it's as safe as the Bank of Demos ...'

Shirna saw a light flickering on the Scope's control-panel, and called Vorg over. 'Another fault,' she whispered. 'In circuit five, this time.'

Vorg was aware of the Officials watching him keenly. 'No doubt some insignificant electrical matter,' he said lightly. 'Switch on the circuit, my dear.'

Shirna obeyed, and everyone crowded to the viewing apertures. Vorg noted sourly that the three Officials, however much they disapproved of the Scope, were as keen as anyone to savour its excitements.

The spectators saw, or rather seemed to be in, a steamy, featureless landscape, a mixture of marshland and swamp. Thick mist drifted across it, and bubbling mud geysers made sinister glugging sounds.

Vorg spoke without looking up. 'It's working perfectly, you see. Nothing wrong at all.'

Shirna looked at the control-panel. 'It's still signalling the alarm.'

Kalik said. 'What do you call the creatures who inhabit this singularly unpleasant landscape?'

A note of real enthusiasm came into Vorg's voice. 'Drashigs, your worship. My little carnivores. Great favourites with the kiddies, they are, snapping and gnashing and tearing at each other ...'

Shirna gave a scream. 'Vorg, *look*!'

Two figures, one small and one tall, had appeared. They were walking uncertainly across the marshlands, looking cautiously around them.

'The new Terrans,' muttered Vorg. 'They've broken into circuit five!'

Shirna gave Vorg one of her nudges. 'You've got to get them out!'

'How can I? They're already as good as dead. Once the Drashigs pick up their scent, they won't stand a chance. They'll be torn to bits.'

'Fascinating,' murmured Kalik. He leaned over his viewing aperture.

After they had been walking for what seemed a very long time, the Doctor stopped and looked about him. The misty marshland stretched all around, exactly the same view in every direction. Every now and again the swamp belched out puffs of stinking marsh-gas. 'This is hopeless, Jo. There's nothing here—certainly not the TARDIS. I don't like the feel of this place.'

Jo shivered, despite the clammy heat. 'Neither do I. Let's go back.' They turned and started to retrace their steps.

At his control-panel viewing aperture, Vorg shook his head sadly. 'They'll never make it ...'

A blood-curdling roar echoed through the swamp. Jo and the Doctor stopped. 'What was that?' Jo whispered.

The Doctor shook his head. 'No idea. But it didn't sound too friendly. Come on, Jo, let's get back to the cave.' The Doctor took the flare pistol from his pocket.

Just ahead, the swamp began to bubble and seethe. A huge blunt head on a long scaly neck burst through the mud. Swinging its head to and fro in search of its prey, the Drashig let out a thunderous bellow . . .

7

'Nothing escapes the Drashigs'

Jo thought she had never seen anything more terrifying in her life. The creature was something between a dinosaur and a dragon with squat body, powerful clawed legs, a sinuous neck and a mouth that seemed to contain not two but at least a dozen rows of enormous razor-edged teeth. The eyes were small and blinking, the nostrils huge and flared.

The monster launched itself across the mud like an express train, hurtling straight towards them. The Doctor raised his flare-pistol in a futile gesture of defiance ... and the monster shot past in a shower of mud, like an express train that wasn't due to stop.

Jo could hardly believe they were still alive. 'Why didn't it attack us, Doctor?'

'I don't think it saw us, Jo. You saw those eyes, and those nostrils. Visibility's poor here and those things have adapted. They must hunt purely by scent. It's still following our outward trail ...'

There were more bellowings, distant, but getting nearer.

'Sounds as if there's more than one of them,' said the Doctor. 'Come on, Jo. We've got to beat that monster back to the cave.'

Shirna looked up from the Scope. 'It's all right, Vorg.

They're escaping.'

Vorg shook his head mournfully. 'Nothing escapes the Drashigs. Even miniaturised they terrify me.'

Pletrac looked up, shaken by what he had seen. 'How many of these—Drashigs are there?'

'Oh, just a small colony—twenty or so!'

'And where do they come from?'

'One of the satellites of Grundle.' Vorg lowered his voice impressively. 'It is said that many years ago a battle-thruster was forced to land there for emergency repairs. It had a crew of fifty, all the latest armament. They thought they could stand off the Drashigs while they fixed the ship.'

'What happened?' asked Pletrac, fascinated despite himself.

'Nothing more was heard of them, so a spy-orbiter was sent to scan the planet. The pictures showed almost nothing left of the battle-thruster. It had been eaten. And as for the crew ...'

Even Kalik was impressed. 'Eaten? They *ate* a spaceship?'

'Apart from a few scraps of the reactor ventricle. The Drashigs are omnivores, you see. Their digestions can cope with anything. Mind you,' added Vorg, 'they prefer flesh when they can get it.'

Jo and the Doctor were running through the swamp. The bellowing of the Drashigs came from all around, and it was getting closer. They were being encircled ...

A roaring Drashig burst out of the swamp ahead of them. Then another ... and another!

Jo and the Doctor stood quite still. The Drashigs

waved their heads to and fro, searching, peering with their little eyes, sniffing with their huge nostrils.

'Doctor, they'll see us in a minute,' whispered Jo. 'That or pick up our scent. If they all charge at once ...'

The Doctor knew she was right. They might hope to dodge *one* of the short-sighted monsters, but never three ...

The Doctor felt the weight of the flare-pistol in his hand. A puny weapon against three such terrors—and yet ...

There was another eruption beneath the swamp, another whiff of stinking marsh-gas. The Doctor sniffed, analysing the contents of that smell. 'Mostly hydrogen,' he muttered. 'Should be highly flammable ...'

Then everything happened at once.

The three Drashigs caught their scent together. All three bellowed and charged.

There was another eruption of marsh-gas just in front of the charging Drashigs. The Doctor fired the flare-pistol into the heart of it.

The marsh-gas eruption turned into a volcano of flame, enveloping the Drashigs. Bellowing in rage and pain, they turned and fled, hiding from the flames beneath the swamp-mud.

The Doctor threw aside the empty flare pistol. They turned and ran for the cave.

It came in sight at last. Just as they began a stumbling run for its entrance, another Drashig burst from the mud, barring their way. And this monster did see them. It opened its mouth, roared terrifyingly and charged. This time there was no marsh-gas and no flare-pistol to save them.

Kalik looked accusingly at Vorg. 'It is your duty to help the Terrans.'

'Me, your worship?' Vorg backed away. 'Put my hand inside—with the Drashigs?'

'You are in charge of the machine. It is your responsibility.'

'Oh, go *on*,' urged Shirna. 'We can't let them be torn to pieces.'

The Drashig was opening its mouth to swallow the Doctor and Jo when a giant hand appeared from the sky and batted it away. The Drashig flew through the air, to land splashing and roaring some distance away. The hand hurriedly withdrew, and the Doctor and Jo sprinted for the cave.

Once they were safely inside, Jo gasped. 'That hand, Doctor ...'

'We'll discuss that later,' said the Doctor hurriedly. 'Let's get back into the machine.' He helped Jo through the little gap at the back of the cave.

They wriggled back down the air duct and started moving through the machine once more. When they came to a fairly open space between two huge circuits, Jo sank to the ground. 'Sorry, Doctor, I've just got to have a rest.'

The Doctor sat down beside her. 'I seem to be feeling the centuries a little myself.'

Jo yawned. 'That swamp we were in? It wasn't the real outside, was it?'

'No. It was another simulated environment. Just like the ship.'

'Isn't it about time you told me where we are, Doctor?'

The Doctor sighed. He'd have to break it to her sooner or later. 'We're inside a MiniScope, Jo—Scope, for short.'

'Inside a what?'

'You remember what I was saying about a boy with a bucket? And you've seen those glass cases people keep colonies of ants in?'

Jo gave him a horrified look. 'You mean Major Daly and all those people on the ship are specimens, in some kind of peepshow? And outside there are people—creatures—looking at them just for kicks? That's terrible!'

'Well, thoughtless, maybe,' said the Doctor gently. 'Did you ever visit a zoo? Keep a goldfish in a glass bowl?'

'That's different! We're not animals!'

'We are to the people out there, Jo.' The Doctor gave a very fair imitation of a showman's patter. 'Roll up, roll up. See these fascinating little animals in their native habitat. Watch their funny tricks, poke 'em with a stick and make 'em jump.'

'Stop it, Doctor! It isn't funny.'

'I agree with you, Jo,' said the Doctor seriously. 'In fact I had a great deal to do with getting these Mini-Scopes banned. I persuaded the Time Lords they were an offence against the dignity of sentient life-forms.'

'I thought the Time Lords never interfered?'

The Doctor chuckled. 'They don't usually. I refused to shut up until they agreed to have Scopes outlawed by Intergalactic Convention. Officially they were all called in and shut down.'

'So how come we're inside one?'

'Somehow this must have been missed. And unfortunately the TARDIS materialised inside its compression-field.'

Jo sighed. 'So here we are, all nicely wrapped up with the other specimens.'

The Doctor clapped her on the shoulder. 'Cheer up Jo. We'll get out of here.'

An echoing roar in the distance brought them both to their feet. They hurried on their way.

Outside the cave in the swamplands, about half-a-dozen Drashigs were milling savagely about. Fighting and clawing each other, they poured into the cave. Struggling in the confined space, they made for the open hatchway in the rear.

Shirna glanced up from the Scope. 'Vorg, come and look. Some of the Drashigs are trying to follow the Terrans.'

Vorg looked and shuddered. 'I should have known. Drashigs never leave a scent—not with any kind of meal at the end of it.'

'Suppose they get out of the circuit, Vorg? Anything could happen.' Shirna lowered her voice to a terrified whisper. 'They might even get out of the Scope.'

Vorg looked round uneasily. 'You keep your thoughts to yourself, my girl. We're in quite enough trouble already!'

The first Drashig found the hatchway at the end of the cave too small. Seizing the edge of the metal in its mighty jaws, it ripped at it like someone opening a sardine can. Slavering ferociously it enlarged the hole, tearing off great chunks of the heavy metal. When the space was big enough, it squeezed through, roaring triumphantly. More Drashigs followed. The terrifying chorus of their howls reached Jo and the Doctor as they staggered ant-like through the interior of the machine, desperately looking for a way out. Behind them they could hear the monsters coming even closer. They broke into a tired run.

'We've got one advantage, Jo,' said the Doctor encouragingly, as they squeezed past a piston. 'We're smaller than they are.'

'That's an advantage?'

'Well, at least we can make better time in these narrow spaces.'

Just as the Doctor spoke they came to a dead end. A Drashig bellowed behind them. 'Start climbing, Jo.' ordered the Doctor. A chain led into the darkness above them. They started to climb it, using the huge links like the rungs of a ladder.

The Doctor swung himself on to the top of a valve casing, and pulled Jo after him. From below came echoing roars as the ferociously determined Drashigs ranged round seeking their prey.

'They'll find a way up here soon,' said Jo hopelessly. Those things never give up.'

'Then neither shall we,' said the Doctor. 'Come on, Jo. We're not done for yet.'

After ages of twisting and turning and clambering through the cramped spaces between the machinery, they seemed to leave the Drashigs behind for at least a while. They came to a horizontal shaft, stretching beneath them like a great canyon. 'Logically, there's an extractor at the bottom of that shaft,' said the Doctor. 'That really will lead to the outside.'

Jo peered over the edge. 'Too far to jump, too smooth to climb. Now what?'

There came more bellows from behind. The Drashigs were still on the trail.

The Doctor had produced pencil and paper and was trying to work out a rough sketch-map of the inside of the Scope. 'We need a bit of lateral thinking, Jo.'

'What's that?'

'A sort of sideways approach. You use it when there aren't any logical answers.' The Doctor pointed to his map. 'You see we can't go forward because of the drop and we can't go back because——'

More shattering roars, nearer this time, made it unnecessary for him to finish.

'I get it,' said Jo, 'we just go sideways.'

'Don't be so literal, Jo. If we go sideways,' the Doctor peered at his map again, 'we'll end up back on the ship.'

'There you are then,' said Jo triumphantly. 'There's rope on the ship. I saw coils of it in the hold. We'll use the rope to get down the shaft. You're brilliant, Doctor.'

'I am?'

Jo grinned. 'Lateral thinking—when in doubt, go sideways!'

Clambering across the circuits and squeezing in and out of narrow spaces, they finally came upon one of the octagonal plates through which they'd first entered the machine:

The Doctor wriggled up the access shaft and opened it with the core-extractor. He slid the hatch back and peered through. To his surprise and delight, he had come up not outside Daly's cabin but in the hold itself. 'Here's a piece of luck, Jo,' he called. 'We've arrived in just the right place.' He helped her through the hatch and they made their way over to the coils of rope.

'How much do we need?' whispered Jo.

'One of these bigger coils should do.'

The roar of a hungry Drashig came from below them.

The Doctor slipped the coil of rope over his shoulder. 'Come on, Jo. I don't think there's much time.'

Light streamed in as the hatchway to the deck was thrown open. Jo caught a glimpse of feet descending, and the Doctor dragged her into hiding. She heard the voice of Lieutenant Andrews. 'Can't see anything wrong here, sir.'

Major Daly's voice said, 'Heard it plainly, I tell you. Sounded just like the Hound of the bally Baskervilles!'

'You're sure it came from the hold, sir?'

'Positive, old boy. Positive.'

'Maybe some of the cargo's shifted,' suggested Andrews. 'Made some kind of groaning as it rolled ...' He glanced round the hold, looking for anything out of place. Then he spotted something. A projecting foot.

'Oh well, best forget it,' said Daly. 'Must be hearin' things, what? Too long at sea. Thank goodness it's Bombay tomorrow. Gad, I look forward to a tub of fresh water. The old briny might be all right for fish ...'

Using Daly's chatter as cover, Andrews crept forward until he was close enough to leap on Jo and drag her from her hiding place.

Daly was astonished. 'I say, a little Memsahib!' he exclaimed. He showed no sign of recognising her.

'All right,' said Andrews grimly. 'When did you stow away?'

Jo sighed. 'Here we go again!'

Andrews took her by the arm. 'You'd better come with us!'

The Doctor was hiding quite close to Jo but, content with his capture, Andrews made no attempt to search further. The Doctor considered rescuing her, but decided against it, at least for the moment. The job of going into the Drashig-infested Scope and climbing down the shaft was one he'd as soon tackle alone. Now that they were out of their artificially induced aggressive state, there was little danger that the people on the ship would harm her. Once he himself was free, he'd find some safe way to get her out. The Doctor started gathering up coils of rope.

Jo was taken to the saloon, allowed to sit down and given a glass of orange squash which she downed gratefully. The atmosphere this time was quite friendly. Her arrival seemed to be regarded as an amusing curiosity.

Clare Daly poured her another glass of squash. 'Why don't you tell John how you got on board?' she said. 'He's really quite nice, you know.'

'I'm sure he is,' said Jo. 'But I'm afraid he'd never believe me.' She looked curiously at Clare. 'How long have you been on this ship?'

'Nearly four weeks, why?'

Jo leaned forward. 'Doesn't it ever seem like ages? Don't you ever feel you've been doing the same things time and time again?'

For a long moment Clare stared at her. It seemed as if some memory might be breaking through. Then she shook her head almost angrily. 'I'm sorry. I just don't know what you mean.'

Jo smiled. 'Never mind,' she said gently.

Andrews came into the room. 'The Captain wants to see you, young lady.'

Jo got up. 'Oh well, anything for a change.'

Andrews was puzzled by her attitude. 'He's certain to put you under arrest,' he warned.

'Last time he was too busy to even see me.'

Andrews too stared curiously at her, as if haunted by some fugitive memory. 'Last time?'

A Drashig roar, now terrifyingly close, interrupted them. Daly turned to Andrews. 'You see, my boy, I was right. There *was* something in the hold!' The two men ran from the room.

His rope in a coil over his shoulder, the Doctor was about to leave by the octagonal hatch when he also heard the roar. It was no more than a few feet away.

The roar came again, and then again. A Drashig thrust its head through the steel wall of the hull, like a circus animal bursting through a paper hoop.

8

The Battle on the Ship

The many-fanged head weaved round in the darkness of the hold. The beady short-sighted eyes focused on the Doctor, and the Drashig hurled itself forwards with a roar.

The Doctor dodged to one side, the hatchway was flung open, and Andrews, Daly and half-a-dozen seamen, all armed with rifles, found themselves staring straight at the charging Drashig.

'I don't believe it,' spluttered Daly.

Andrews was more practical. 'Fire!' he yelled.

Andrews and Daly led the seamen in a ragged volley. Screaming with pain and rage the Drashig hurled itself bodily across the hold and burst out of the hatch on to the deck, scattering men to all sides. In its progress it knocked down a pile of crates, most of which landed on top of the Doctor.

Andrews and Daly picked themselves up and made for the saloon, where Clare and Jo were waiting terrified. 'Did you see the Doctor?' called Jo.

Andrews ignored her. 'You stay here, Major,' he called. 'Look after the ladies.'

Andrews ran out on deck. The Drashig had made its way forward and was rampaging across the decks. The Captain and a grim-faced group of seamen stood by with rifles, waiting for a shot at it.

As Andrews arrived, a seaman came running up with

a heavy Thompson sub-machine gun. The Captain took it. 'Now we should be able to settle it,' he said. 'This thing'll stop anything!'

'I know where there's something even more useful, sir,' called Andrews. 'Dynamite, in the aft hold.'

'Good man,' said the Captain. 'See what you can do.' Andrews dashed away.

The Drashig changed its course and started moving towards them. Daly stuck his head out of the saloon window and called to the Captain. 'Take cover here, sir. We can fire through the window.'

The Captain ran into the saloon with the machine gun. Daly already had the saloon portholes thrown wide open. Clare and Jo were sheltering behind a sofa. Daly immediately took charge, with the assurance of an old military man. It was ten years since he'd seen action on the Western Front, but he was still ready to do his best. Firmly he took the sub-machine gun from the Captain. 'If you'll just let me have that, sir, I'll take the main charge here, and you can post your riflemen out on deck, some each side of the saloon.'

The Captain nodded and ran out. Daly waited grim-faced as the Drashig's roars came nearer. Suddenly the monster's slavering head appeared at the saloon window. Clare screamed. Daly fired a long raking burst with the sub-machine gun, pouring the entire magazine of .45 calibre bullets into the Drashig's body. At the same time the Captain and crew were firing their rifles into its flanks.

Not even a Drashig could stand up to such a hail of bullets. Torn almost to pieces the monster lurched back roaring, and collapsed on the edge of the deck. The weight of the body smashed through the deck-rails, and the dying monster slithered slowly into the sea. Everyone stopped shooting, and an uncanny silence fell. Only the blood-stained bullet-torn deck showed that a battle had just taken place.

In the hold, the Doctor, half-stunned, was struggling from beneath his pile of crates. He saw a kneeling figure crouched over a wooden box, breaking the wire binding round the lid. It was Andrews.

There came a shattering roar. Another Drashig was forcing its way through the shattered wall.

Andrews spun round and lit the fuse on a stick of dynamite. The Doctor struggled to his feet. 'No, don't. You'll wreck the Scope and kill us all.'

Andrews hurled the sputtering dynamite stick at the Drashig. The dynamite exploded in mid-air, blowing the monster back down the shaft. Andrews lit a second stick, threw it, then turned and ran from the hold. The second stick of dynamite went off halfway down the shaft, exploding devastatingly in the confined space. There was a brilliant white flash and a prolonged roar. The Doctor went to the gap. Smoke was drifting upwards, and molten metal trickled down the walls. 'Oh dear,' said the Doctor, 'now that's really done it!'

He wondered again about going back for Jo, but decided against it. Judging from the silence, the Drashigs were beaten off for the moment. Jo would be far safer where she was than where he was going. Settling the rope round his shoulders, the Doctor opened the octagonal hatch and began to climb down the shaft.

Jo was just about to slip out of the saloon and look for the Doctor when Daly came back from his inspection of the deck.

'Sorry about all the fuss, my dear,' he said calmly. 'I'm sure the Captain won't keep you very long. By Jove, that beast took a bit of stopping, eh? Think we all deserve a chota peg, what?' Suiting the action to the word, Daly poured himself a stiff drink.

Clare looked up shuddering. 'What a terrible beast. I've never seen anything like it, have you?'

Daly shook his head solemnly.

'Well, I have,' said Jo. 'There are quite a lot of them about.'

Daly nodded. 'Strange waters, these, my dear. Always said so.'

Jo suddenly became impatient with the banal conversation. She tried to slip past Daly, but he put out a restraining arm, blocking the doorway. 'Please let me go,' she said pleadingly. 'I've got to find the Doctor.'

'Feeling a bit umpty,' said Daly sympathetically. 'Not surprising after all you've been through. We'll get the ship's Doctor to take a look at you soon.'

'Not the ship's Doctor,' said Jo. '*My* Doctor—oh, never mind!'

Andrews came into the saloon. He had changed into a fresh uniform, and was his old immaculate self. Daly looked up. 'Hullo, old chap, sundowner?'

Clare looked up, her face calm and composed again. 'Daddy, John and I are going for a walk round the deck.'

Andrews smiled. 'That's right. Twenty times round the deck is a mile. Coming, Clare?'

Jo stared at them with a mixture of amusement and horror. They were settling calmly back into their old grooves again. Things weren't exactly the same, but near enough. No doubt everything would soon be back to its unvarying normal. 'You've forgotten everything, haven't you?' she burst out.

Daly turned and stared at her, whisky-glass in hand. ''Pon my soul!'

'And who might you be?' demanded Andrews sternly.

Jo looked at him defiantly. 'How do you know I'm not a passenger? None of you can remember anything of more than ten minutes back—so how do you know?' Jo could feel herself getting hysterical. She stared wildly round the saloon. 'Can't you remember me?' she asked. 'Don't you remember fighting that monster?'

Clare Daly gave her a pitying look. 'I'm sorry. I don't know what you're talking about.'

'Monster? What monster?' Daly chuckled. 'Seen the sea-serpent, have you?'

'We were attacked by a monster,' said Jo desperately. 'I was with you when you shot it down ...' Before any of them could stop her, she rushed blindly from the saloon.

Daly drained his drink and poured another. 'Poor gel. Must be suffering from a touch of the sun.'

Andrews nodded. 'Still, can't have stowaways running about. I'd better round her up.'

As he walked from the saloon, Daly called. 'Look out for the monster, old chap!'

Clare smiled to herself. Monsters! Of all the absurd ideas.

Pletrac, Kalik and Orum were engaged in yet another

of their unending conferences on the subject of Vorg
and Shirna and their Scope. Kalik, as usual, was being
awkward. 'According to law, the Lurmans should be
deported and their specimens destroyed.'

It was Orum who asked the unanswerable question.
'How?'

'How indeed,' agreed Pletrac. 'Since the Eradicator
has no effect, we should deport both Lurmans *and*
machine.'

'That is not within the authority of this Tribunal,'
objected Kalik. 'To do that you must obtain special
powers from President Zarb.'

Pletrac sighed wearily. 'That will take some time.'

'No doubt. But it is the correct procedure.'

Pletrac sighed wearily. 'Very well, I will seek special
powers from Zarb. Make sure the Eradicator Functionaries remain alert.' Pletrac bustled away. Kalik smiled
—and Orum stared wonderingly at him.

Over by the Scope, Shirna was looking at a flashing
light on the control panel. 'Vorg, there's another fault
signalled.'

Vorg shrugged. 'A minor blockage in one of the feed
lines. It'll correct itself.'

'That minor blockage is probably a Drashig,' said
Shirna. 'Look!' She switched over to circuit five. The
area round the cave in the marshes was completely
deserted. 'See—not a Drashig in sight.'

'Nothing unusual in that.' Vorg's voice was defensive. 'The little dears are shy.'

'You know what they're like, Vorg. They mill
around for hours after a kill. Some of those Drashigs
are loose inside the Scope. They're roaming around
out of their circuit!'

A cold voice spoke from behind them. 'The machine has become dangerous in some way?' It was Kalik. Orum, as ever, at his side, both had slipped up quietly.

Vorg waved a dismissive hand. 'Oh no, your worship, not at all.'

'Oh, tell 'em the truth,' said Shirna wearily. 'What does it matter now? We think some of the Drashigs have broken out of their circuit. They followed the Terrans into the cave and they haven't come out again.'

'Where does the cave lead?'

Shirna said, 'Down into the supply lines. There's a control valve at the back.'

'Well,' said Vorg angrily. 'If the Drashigs have got out—and I'm not saying for a moment they have—whose suggestion was it that I should help the Terrans to escape, eh, Shirna?'

'Mine!' said Kalik.

'And a most merciful and compassionate suggestion too, your worship,' said Vorg swiftly.

Orum looked strangely at Kalik. 'Merciful and compassionate? You, Kalik?'

Kalik smiled coldly. 'One has twinges.'

Orum and Kalik strolled up to one of the Official ramps, and stood viewing the busy Spaceport. There was no one near them. Quietly Orum said, 'You expect these Drashigs to follow the escaping Terrans?'

'They follow a scent for ever, never give up. Or so Vorg tells us. If the Terrans escape from the machine, the Drashigs will follow them.'

'What is to be gained by that?'

'Possibly the world.' Kalik's voice was low and fanatical. 'Ever since the great Space Plague, we have stood alone and been strong. Now Zarb is changing our ways.'

Orum protested. 'But the Functionaries are restless. Perhaps we need change.'

'What we need, Orum, is something to unite us. We need a leader—and we need a war!'

'And who will give us all this?'

'I will,' said Kalik quietly. 'By leading a rebellion against my brother Zarb.'

9

Kalik Plans Rebellion

Although there was no one near by, Orum looked anxiously about him. 'Zarb's position is secure ... how will you achieve rebellion?'

'Suppose these Drashigs escape from the Scope and cause havoc in the City? Who would be blamed? President Zarb! The Scope and the Drashigs are here only because of his liberal policies.'

'No doubt ill feeling would spring up—with a little calculated encouragement. But you forget the Eradicator. Once they leave the Scope's protective force-field, the Eradicator can destroy the Drashigs with ease.'

Kalik nodded. 'True, Orum. *If* it is in working order. Come!'

Kalik led the way down the ramp. He strolled up to the Eradicator Functionaries and dismissed them. Since they were mere Functionaries, and he was an Official, they obeyed without question.

He turned to Orum. 'You have technical knowledge. Remove some small but vital part.'

Nervously Orum slipped behind the Eradicator, returning moments later with a serrated crystal strip. 'This is the Tryizon Focuser. The Eradicator is useless without it.'

They had achieved their piece of sabotage just in time. Pletrac came bustling back across the Spaceport.

'President Zarb has granted our tribunal the special powers,' he announced importantly. 'The two Lurmans and their Scope are to be deported. A special Transporter is being arranged.'

Kalik pointed to the TARDIS. 'And the Terran container?'

'That will be deported too, and jettisoned in deep space.'

Suddenly Pletrac noticed that the Eradicator was unguarded. 'Where are the Functionaries?'

'In the guard block,' said Kalik. 'One relieved them of duty. They appeared fatigued.'

Pletrac turned to Orum. 'Fetch them at once!' Orum scurried away. 'You have exceeded your authority, Kalik,' Pletrac went on. 'There will be an inquiry. Is that clear?'

'Perfectly, Chairman Pletrac. Perfectly clear.' With an insolent nod, Kalik strolled across the Spaceport towards the alcove with the Scope. He saw Vorg and Shirna leaning over it, and moved quietly closer, finally reaching a position behind a pillar where he could listen unobserved.

'Look at all these dials, Vorg,' he heard Shirna say.

Then Vorg's voice. 'What about them?'

'They're suddenly dropping lower, all of them. It's a general power failure.'

Vorg stared at the dials, shaking his head unbelievingly. 'The generators were built by the old Eternity Perpetuity company. Designed to last for ever—that's why the company went bankrupt!' He bent over the dials, adjusting the controls. 'Something pretty drastic must have happened in there,' he grumbled. 'It'd take an explosion to do this much damage . . .'

Shirna watched him. 'Those dials are still dropping. They'll soon be down to critical point.'

Vorg looked up. 'There should be enough power in the circuits to keep them ticking over for a while.'

'Long enough to repair it?'

'Perhaps. If only I hadn't lost the manual ...'

Shirna gave him a disgusted look, and Kalik stepped out of hiding. The Scope was a vital part of his plan, and he didn't want anything going wrong with it—not yet, at any rate. Not until those Drashigs had escaped. 'What is the matter?' he asked.

Vorg gave a guilty start. 'Oh, just routine maintenance, your worship.'

'I have reconsidered my position,' said Kalik, lying smoothly. 'I have made a recommendation that you be allowed to stay. President Zarb is favourably considering it. However, if your machine is no longer in working order ...'

'A minor fault, your worship, nothing more. I shall repair it at once.' Vorg leaped towards the tool-bag.

But the damage to the Scope was far beyond repair —as the Doctor could have witnessed. Picking his way through the complex machine's interior, he was appalled at the amount of destruction. The explosion of Andrews's dynamite seemed to have set off a chain reaction. All around him, the great metal shapes were twisted and warped. The steady pulsing glow of the valves had become an erratic flickering, and the low hum of power an agonised groan.

Stretched across one circuit, the Doctor found the charred body of a Drashig. The creature had bitten through a power cable, and had paid the penalty. No doubt there were more of them roaming the works, doing incalculable damage, as their savage teeth chewed through metal and plastic.

The Doctor reached the steep shaft he had found with Jo. He tied the end of his rope to a cross strut, tossed the coil over the edge, and began descending hand over hand into the depths.

Down and down the Doctor went, into the darkness of the shaft. Soon he was encouraged by a faint glow of light at the very bottom. But before he reached it, the Doctor's luck, and his rope, ran out. Swinging on the end of the rope, the Doctor thought hard.

He could climb all the way up the rope, go back to the ship, get more rope, then come down again ... the thought of going through all that was intolerable, not to mention the risks of being eaten by a Drashig or recaptured by the ship's crew. Moreover, he was tiring now. He doubted if he had the strength to make it to the top again.

The Doctor took a calculated risk. According to his own estimations he must be fairly near the bottom by now—and there was only one way to find out. He flexed his knees, and let go of the rope.

The fall was a surprisingly short one. He bent his legs as he hit the bottom, and rolled over on one shoulder like a parachutist. Picking himself up, he looked about. He was in a dark and empty space with metal walls, like an aircraft hangar. He guessed that he was now underneath the machinery, and in the very bottom of the Scope. He looked around and saw the gleam of light he had spotted from the shaft, and ran towards it.

The gleam came from a slight gap caused by the buckling of a metal base-plate. It was—just—wide enough to let him through. The Doctor started squeezing through the gap.

He was so intent on getting out, that he gave little thought to what he might find on the other side. Not until he was through the gap did he straighten up and look around.

The spectacle was terrifying. High, high above him disappearing into nothingness rose a sheer metal cliff —the outside wall of the Scope. He was in a vast open space through which moved giant forms pushing enormous metal objects. Dizzy, the Doctor spun round. Some huge shape was dominating the landscape before him. There was something familiar about it. Suddenly the Doctor realised what it was. He was looking at a giant golden boot! The boot rose and came down, and the Doctor realised he was in danger of being crushed like an ant.

He ran into the middle of the echoing confusion, desperate to escape. But his legs were giving way beneath him, and his head was spinning round. He stumbled and fell . . .

The appearance of the Doctor from the Scope caused an even bigger sensation than the arrival of the TARDIS before him. No one had noticed the ant-like figure emerge from the base of the Scope. But released from the Scope's compression-field it started to grow . . . and grow . . . and grow . . .

There was panic, Functionaries were fleeing in all directions . . .

When the Doctor grew only to normal size, and did

nothing more threatening than lay on the floor unconscious, the panic died down.

Vorg, Shirna and the three Minoran Officials gath-
ered round the body. The Doctor began to stir, and
Pletrac jumped back in panic. 'Eradicator, Eradicator!' he shouted in alarm. The Eradicator Functionaries had made off, and Pletrac ran to fetch them back.

The Doctor struggled to a sitting position. He looked
round, relieved to find himself normal size again. Leaning over him were two humanoids in tattered gold
finery, one female and one male.

Two male humanoids in grey robes were hovering
near by.

Shirna put an arm round the Doctor's shoulders, and
helped him to get up. 'Feeling better, dear?' she said
brightly, and the Doctor grinned at the homely re-
mark. He stood up, swaying a little—and found himself looking into the mouth of an electronic cannon.
A grey-robed humanoid, an older white-haired one
this time, was giving orders to the brutish uniformed
figures manning the gun.

Vorg and Shirna jumped back instinctively. 'Leave
him alone,' shouted Shirna. 'He hasn't done anything.
It's one of the Terrans from the Scope.'

'It must be eradicated at once,' ordered Pletrac. 'Get
away from it—it's probably crawling with alien
germs!'

Swaying a little the Doctor now stood alone, the
Eradicator trained on him at point-blank range. Still
half-unaware of his danger, he was trying to make
sense of the noise and confusion around him.

He heard Vorg's voice. 'Come away, Shirna, the
noble master is right. The thing must be destroyed.'

He heard Pletrac's command. 'Detachment! One charge at maximum intensity! Fire!'

Too weak to dodge or to run, the Doctor looked straight down the muzzle of the Eradicator.

10

The Doctor Takes Over

As the Eradicator Functionary's finger was about to descend on the firing button, a thin, grey-robed figure stepped between the Doctor and the muzzle of the cannon. Raising his hand, Kalik said, 'Stop!'

The Functionary snatched his hand away. To fire upon an Official would be unthinkable. Kalik exchanged a swift glance with the tubby Orum, who was hovering as usual on the sidelines. As they both knew, the Doctor was really in no danger whatsoever since the Eradicator had been sabotaged. But if Kalik's plan was to succeed this must not be discovered until the Drashigs burst out of the Scope. Therefore, the Eradicator must not be fired before then, and the Doctor had to be saved. Kalik had taken his action on impulse. Now his agile brain was looking for ways to justify it.

Pletrac hurried up, gobbling with rage. 'Stand aside, Kalik!'

Kalik did not move. 'This procedure is not in order. The Eradicator cannot be used without authority from President Zarb.'

'But surely in an emergency . . .'

'One alien does not constitute an emergency.'

'The function of our tribunal is to keep this planet clean. The Terran creature is from outside our Solar system and is a possible carrier of contagion. Furthermore, the creature may well be hostile.'

The Doctor was recovering fast now, and he was becoming rather tired of being discussed as though he wasn't there. He marched up to Pletrac and said, 'Kindly stop referring to me as "the creature", sir, or I may well *become* exceedingly hostile!'

Pletrac jumped away from the tall figure. 'Silence, alien. The tribunal is deliberating.'

'The tribunal is *not* deliberating, it is wrangling. And quite nonsensically too, if I may say so!'

Pletrac was outraged. 'I warn you, this tribunal will not tolerate insolent remarks from unauthorised alien life-forms!'

Changing his tack, the Doctor smiled down at the fussy little Official. 'I wonder if you'd be kind enough to tell me exactly where I am? What planet, I mean?'

'You are on Inter Minor,' said Pletrac importantly. Surely this would impress the alien.

The Doctor looked dejected. 'Not Metebelis Three, famous blue planet of the Acteon Galaxy?' he inquired sadly.

'No.'

The Doctor sighed, abandoning all hopes of winning his argument with Jo. 'Ah well, never mind.' He walked over to the TARDIS, and gave the blue box a pat. 'Well, at least you're all right, old girl.'

Pletrac and the other Officials had followed him. 'This container is yours?' demanded Pletrac.

'It is indeed,' said the Doctor. Standing near the TARDIS he saw another shape—a tall cylinder on legs, viewing apertures around the sides. He strode across to it. 'Just as I thought. A MiniScope!' He whirled round on Pletrac. 'This is outrageous! Is this disgraceful device yours?'

So angry was the Doctor's tone that Pletrac found himself replying defensively. 'Certainly not. It is the property of the Lurman entertainer here. The female is his assistant.'

The Doctor turned his stern gaze on the two entertainers in their shabby gold finery. He saw Shirna's worried face and remembering her earlier kindness, made a courtly bow. Shirna curtsied back, suppressing a nervous giggle.

The Doctor returned his attention to Pletrac, 'I see. Well, I'll deal with them later. And you are?'

'Chairman Pletrac of the Alien Admissions Tribunal. One's colleagues are Commissioner Kalik and Commissioner Orum.'

Apparently addressing the air, Kalik said, 'One wonders why the Tribunal is submitting to questioning by the alien, instead of questioning it? Surely that is the wrong way round?'

It took more than a little sarcasm to worry the Doctor. He looked severely at the three grey-robed Commissioners. 'Well, gentlemen, I'm sorry to have to tell you that you are in very serious trouble.'

Orum shook his head. 'One is forced to admire the creature's audacity.'

Kalik said nothing. He was weighing up the Doctor, wondering how he could best make use of him.

The Doctor's own behaviour had been calculated from the very first. As long as Jo Grant was inside the Scope, she was still in great danger. There was simply no time for all the nonsense of imprisonment and interrogation that usually followed unexplained arrival on some alien planet. He had to dominate these Minorans from the start, force them to help him.

Nothing less than Jo's life was at stake.

He gave Chairman Pletrac another unnerving frown. 'I take it you and your Commission are representatives of authority on this planet?'

'One's authority comes direct from President Zarb,' said Pletrac proudly.

The Doctor promptly deflated him. 'Then yours is the responsibility. You have allowed the importation —and operation—of a device expressly forbidden by Intergalactic Law.'

'One did not allow it,' protested Pletrac. 'One has already ordered the deportation of the entertainers and their machine.'

The Doctor sighed wearily. His manner was that of some High Court Judge, all too used to seeing petty criminals trying to wriggle out of their responsibilities. 'Nevertheless, the machine *is* here—and it *is* in operation. You'll scarcely deny that?'

Confused, Pletrac stammered, 'Well ... strictly speaking, one is forced to concede the fact that ... in a sense ...'

The Doctor cut ruthlessly through the waffle. 'Precisely. As a direct result of your carelessness, my young female companion is still inside that device, in a situation of extreme peril.'

Pletrac made an attempt to fight back. 'One is forced to remind you, alien, that the question before this Tribunal is your own possible eradication as a menace to public health.'

The Doctor went on as if Pletrac hadn't spoken. 'If you'll allow me to rescue my companion, and do something for the other unfortunates imprisoned in that disgraceful device—I'm prepared to overlook the whole unfortunate business.'

'One is indeed overwhelmed,' said Kalik dryly.

The Doctor turned his back on them. 'If not—well, you'll just have to take the consequences. Let me know when you've made up your minds.' Folding his arms the Doctor gazed into space, as if the whole debate was of only minimal interest to him. But beneath his apparent calm, he was in a turmoil, wondering if his bluff would work. His experienced eyes had summed up the Minorans very quickly. He was gambling that like all authoritarians, they would harass and bully anyone who seemed weaker than themselves, while responding favourably to a display of force and bluster.

As the Doctor waited, Vorg and Shirna were observing him. There was an expression of tremendous admiration on Vorg's face. Himself a born coward, terrified by all authority, he was lost in wonder at the way this tall, elegant figure had dealt with the Officials. 'Marvellous,' he breathed. 'What audacity! You know, Shirna, I do believe he's one of us!'

'One of us? He's a Terran, isn't he?'

'The brotherhood of showmen is Intergalactic,' said Vorg loftily. 'He's *got* to be in the carnival business, Shirna. Look at his manner, look at his clothes. I recognise the type, I tell you. I've worked many a Terran fairground.'

Shirna looked wistfully at the Doctor. 'You may be right. He's certainly got style.'

'I'd lay a wager on it. He's got the measure of those grey-faced fools right enough.' Somehow Vorg drew courage from the Doctor's defiance of Officialdom.

As usual the Official conference had ended in disagreement. Pletrac was for eradicating the Doctor at once on grounds of general hygiene. Kalik was desperate to stop any attempt to use the Eradicator, and Orum, as usual, followed Kalik.

'Admit it, Pletrac,' said Kalik. 'You are outvoted.'

As a good Official Pletrac had no choice but to defer to the decisions of his tribunal. 'Oh, very well.' He waved a hand. 'Eradicator Unit, stand down. But remain here. You may yet be needed.'

The Doctor had observed the decision. With a well-concealed sigh of relief he turned round. 'Thank you, gentlemen.' He bowed to Kalik. 'And thank you, sir, for a most timely intervention.'

As the Doctor turned and strode away, Pletrac called, 'Alien! Where are you going?'

The Doctor paused. 'Just over here, sir. I have work to do.' He moved over to the Scope and started examining it.

Pletrac looked keenly at Kalik. 'One confesses one is puzzled, Kalik. What use is this Terran to you?'

Kalik was wondering the same thing himself, but he shrugged indifferently and said, 'Of no possible use.'

'You never do anything without a reason, Kalik. One is wondering why you bothered to save the Terran's life.'

Kalik gave his cold smile. 'Out of mercy and compassion, Pletrac. Vorg will tell you.' He strolled away, Orum at his heels. Pletrac looked after them, worried. He decide to watch and wait. He would also send a message requesting more powers from President Zarb, so as to resolve this intolerable situation.

Vorg and Shirna watched from the background as the tall alien examined the Scope. Despite the fact that the machine was their property, they lacked the courage to protest, or even to ask him what he was doing.

Shirna said, 'Go on, Vorg, offer to help him. Maybe he'll put in a good word for us.'

Vorg plucked up his courage. 'Perhaps you're right. I mean, he *is* a fellow showman ...' An idea struck him. 'Here! I'll just see if he talks the palare.' Vorg was referring to the universal showman's slang, which had spread out from Terra and across the galaxy.

He sidled up to the Doctor and spoke in a low confidential murmur out of the side of his mouth. 'Parlare the carny, mate?'

The Doctor looked up and raised an eyebrow. 'I beg your pardon?'

'Varda the bonapalone?' persisted Vorg.

Unaware that he was being addressed in the secret language of carnival showmen, the Doctor shook his head.

Vorg leaned forward. 'Niente dinari here, y'jils?' said Vorg, warning the Doctor that there was no money to be made on Inter Minor.

The Doctor sighed, and spoke very slowly and clearly. 'I am sorry. I do not understand your language.'

Vorg gave him a nudge. 'Come on, you understand all right. You're a showman, aren't you, just like me?'

The Doctor looked thoughtfully at him, taking in the rather seedy flamboyance of the well-worn costume. 'So you're a showman, are you?'

Vorg swept him a splendid bow. 'Allow me to introduce myself. I am the Great Vorg, renowned Intergalactic Entertainer. This is my assistant, Shirna.'

The Doctor returned the bow. 'Delighted to meet you. I am called the Doctor.'

'That's right,' said Vorg cheerfully. 'Nothing like a title. Doctors, Professors, that always brings in the crowd. I knew you were a showman.'

The Doctor decided it wasn't worth trying to disillusion him. 'I gather you're in charge of this device?'

'That's right. Something wrong?'

'A great deal is wrong. A young friend of mine is still trapped in there, and I've got to find some way of getting her out. Now, where's the inspection-hatch?'

Vorg took it off for him. 'I shouldn't put your hand inside, Doctor. Those Drashigs can take a lump right out of you.'

'Drashigs?' The Doctor frowned. 'I take it that's the name of those creatures that attacked us in the swamp?'

Shirna nodded. 'Trouble is some of them followed you out of their own circuit, and they seem to be running wild inside. Doing terrible damage, aren't they, Vorg?'

Vorg nodded sadly, looking at the flickering display of warning lights on the Scope's control-panel. 'I reckon they've wrecked the stato-fields. I'm probably going to lose the entire collection. Be a real tragedy that would. My insurance doesn't cover replacement of livestock.'

The Doctor looked at him appalled. 'Livestock! Are you aware that there are human beings in there?'

'That's right. Terrans, Ogrons, Drashigs, Cybermen, Ice Warriors—marvellous collection ...'

The Doctor lifted Vorg off his feet and shook him angrily. 'The collection of the simplest animal life-forms is a dubious enough pursuit at best, sir,' he thundered. He gave Vorg another shake, rattling his teeth. 'But the collection of intelligent, civilised life-forms is a positive crime! I warn you, I intend to put an end to this disgraceful machine of yours!' He set Vorg down with a thump.

Vorg backed hurriedly out of reach, smoothing down his lapels. 'No need to get excited,' he said reproach-fully. 'Besides, you needn't worry about the Scope. It's putting an end to itself.'

The Doctor leaned over the control-panel. 'I've been trying to interpret the warning-light display. Can you tell me exactly what it means?'

'The machine's packing up,' said Vorg glumly. 'It's as simple as that. All the life-support systems are going to break down soon.'

'It's just ticking over now,' confirmed Shirna. 'The power level's almost down to critical.'

The Doctor realised things were even worse than he feared. 'How long do you think it will last?'

Vorg shrugged. 'No idea. Can't be much longer.'

The Doctor spoke, almost to himself. 'And when power drops below critical, the artificial life-support systems will fail—and every living creature inside the Scope will die!'

11

Return to Peril

On board the S.S. *Bernice*, the hunt for Jo Grant went
on. There was nothing very serious or dramatic about
it. With the aggrometer turned off the passengers and
crew had long ago reverted to their amiable selves.
They weren't too worried about one very small girl
stowaway. The hunt was conducted rather like a jolly
game of hide and seek, with excited shouts whenever
Jo was spotted and ran to some other hiding place.

Neither Jo nor her pursuers knew of the danger
which loomed over them all. Once the Scope power
dropped below critical, their artificial world would
come to a sudden end. The tropical sun would go out,
there would be no light, no warmth and eventually no
air. Their world, and their lives, would end in choking
darkness.

Hearing the sound of approaching feet, Jo jumped
from the lifeboat where she'd been hiding and sprinted
across the deck. She ran to the chain-locker, pulled it
open and squeezed inside. Her diminutive size was
a great advantage in the game. Several times her pursuers had ignored her hiding places, assuming no one
could squeeze into so small a place.

She heard footsteps on the deck outside the chain-
locker, then Andrews's voice. 'Any sign of her?'

Daly's voice answered. 'Not a bally trace, old boy.'

'Never mind, she's got to be somewhere. We'll just

have to carry on looking.'

The footsteps moved away.

Although the chain-locker was a very good hiding place, it was also cold, dark and damp, and Jo soon got bored with it. She decided to make for the hold. If the Doctor came back to look for her, as she was sure he eventually would, that would be the best place to wait for him.

She slipped out of the locker and crept across the deck. No one was in sight. Andrews and Daly must be searching some other part of the ship. She found a hatchway, opened it and climbed down into the darkness of the hold.

Even in the dim light she could see the devastation left by the Drashig attack. There was a great gaping hole in one wall, and boxes and crates were scattered everywhere. Surely Andrews and the others would notice all this? Or possibly not. Their mental conditioning seemed to block out everything that didn't conform to their picture of ordinary shipboard life.

Jo wondered if the Doctor might still be hiding. Maybe he'd been wounded in the battle with the Drashigs and was lying helpless somewhere. 'Doctor,' she called softly. 'Doctor, are you there?'

Andrews stepped out from behind a pile of crates, grinning broadly. 'Got you, my girl,' he said cheerfully. He moved in front of the ladder, blocking her escape.

'All right,' said Jo. 'I know the routine.'

Sure enough, the routine was exactly the same. She was taken first to the saloon, for a little chat with Major Daly and Clare (both of whom reacted as if they were meeting her for the first time), and then to Daly's cabin.

Andrews unlocked the door and threw it open. 'In you go, my girl. You'll stay here . . .'

'Until the Captain can find time to see me, and it may be some time because he's a very busy man,' chanted Jo. 'All right, I know.'

Andrews gave her a rather puzzled look. 'That's right. Just you be a sensible girl.' He closed and locked the door.

Jo listened to the sound of his retreating footsteps. 'Well, here we go again,' she said. Producing her skeleton keys, she got to work on the door.

Lurking behind their usual pillar. Kalik and Orum watched the Doctor at work on the Scope.

'What is the Terran doing?' asked Orum with his usual mild curiosity.

'Trying to rescue its companion, one imagines,' said Kalik impatiently. The strain of waiting was beginning to get on his nerves. The Drashigs were being uncommonly slow to get out of the Scope and cause the havoc which Kalik needed for the start of his revolution.

The two Lurmans and the Scope were due to be taken off the planet soon. It would be of no use to Kalik if the Drashigs' escape took place on some cargo-rocket. It had to happen here, in the City.

Orum watched fascinatedly as the Doctor, coat off and sleeves rolled up, worked feverishly. 'The Terran is evidently concerned for its companion,' he observed. 'Clearly they are social creatures.'

'And harmless,' added Kalik sourly. It would have

suited his purposes better if the Doctor had fangs and claws.

Orum looked across to the Eradicator, where Pletrac stood obstinately on guard. 'Pletrac is suspicious,' he said, stating the obvious with his usual maddening calm. 'If it occurs to him to check over the Eradicator, he will discover that one has rendered it useless.'

'You worry too much, Orum.'

'Possibly so, Kalik. But President Zarb, liberal as he is, still enforces the death penalty for acts of treason.'

Kalik considered. 'Perhaps, Orum, you have a point,' he conceded. 'Do you have the part you removed from the Eradicator?'

'The Trizon Focuser? Yes, I have it here.'

'Then we shall conceal it in the Vorg's baggage,' said Kalik. 'If anything does go wrong—one of us can always discover it.'

A slow smile spread over Orum's face. 'Brilliant. We shall blame everything on Vorg. Then he will be the one to be executed.'

'Naturally,' said Kalik. 'It is a fitting fate for an alien spy and saboteur.'

They began drifting closer to the Scope.

Vorg was watching worriedly as the Doctor worked, head poked deep inside the Scope's inspection-hatch. 'He could lose that long nose of his, you know, just like that. If there's a Drashig about ...' Vorg made a snapping motion with his fingers.

'Vorg, look!' Shirna pointed downwards. One of the base panels of the Scope was vibrating regularly —as if something was pounding against if from the inside. 'There are Drashigs about all right. Vorg. Down there. They've reached the outer hull of the Scope. If they get out . . . they'll expand to full size and . . .'

Shirna's voice was rising hysterically. Vorg shushed her. 'Come on, my girl, this is where we beat it.'

Shirna hesitated. She was a kind-hearted girl, and felt they ought at least to warn the Doctor. Vorg pulled her away.

'Never mind him. He's so high and mighty, he can look after himself.'

With elaborate casualness, Vorg and Shirna began strolling across the Spaceport. As they neared the Eradicator, Pletrac stepped out, barring their way. 'Where are you going?'

'Ah, well, yes,' said Vorg. He looked appealingly at Shirna. 'Where are we going?'

'Home,' said Shirna firmly.

'Yes, indeed, precisely,' gabbled Vorg. 'We thought we'd find a Lurman freighter and hitch a ride back.'

'That will not be necessary. A special Transporter has been ordered for you—and your Scope.'

Vorg shuddered at the thought of being shut up with a Drashig on a spaceship. 'There's really no need,' he said hurriedly. 'We really don't want to give you any trouble. We'll find our own way home. Tell you what, you can keep the Scope—you're welcome to it.'

'We do not wish to keep the Scope,' said Pletrac severely. 'You—and it—will leave the planet in the special Transporter.'

'It's very kind of you,' said Shirna, 'but really——'

'Not at all,' said Pletrac. Rather tactlessly he added, 'In any case, the Transporter will be disinfected before further use.'

'Disinfected,' said Shirna outraged. 'Now you look here . . .'

Vorg was too worried to bother about minor insults. 'We couldn't think of putting your worships to so much trouble,' he said ingratiatingly. 'So if you'll just let us pass, we'll ...'

With surprising speed for one of his years, Pletrac produced a blaster from beneath his grey robes. 'You will wait until the Transporter arrives,' he commanded.

Vorg groaned. 'Well, of course, if your worship puts it that way ...'

Pletrac waved the blaster. 'You will go back, back, back!' he ordered.

They went back. The plate of the Scope was vibrating more fiercely than ever.

Since his attempt at self-preservation had failed, Vorg decided he might as well do the decent thing. He sidled up to the Doctor. 'I wouldn't stay too close to the Scope if I were you, Doctor. You see, any minute now, the Drashigs are going to ...'

The Doctor didn't seem interested in Vorg's warning. 'There you are, old chap. Now listen. I've managed to patch things up a bit, but the life-support systems won't hold for much longer—there's simply too much damage. I need your help.'

Vorg shied away again. '*My* help? What can *I* do?'

'I've got to go back inside the Scope.'

'What? are you mad, Doctor?'

'It's the only way I can get my friend out of there— and perhaps save the rest of your "livestock" as well. Now then, you'll have to trigger the compression and decompression settings for me, right?'

Vorg tugged agitatedly at his moustache. 'Trigger the what?' he repeated blankly.

The Doctor stared at him. 'This is your machine, isn't it? I presume you do know how it works?'

Dumbly, Vorg shook his head.

The Doctor looked from Vorg to Shirna appalled. Shirna said, 'He won it, Doctor.'

'He *won* the Scope?'

'That's right,' confirmed Vorg. 'It was at the Great Wallarian Exhibition. You know what crazy gamblers those Wallarians are? Well, I had the magum pod concession.'

The Doctor ran his fingers through his hair, wondering if the strain was affecting his mind. 'Magum pod?' he said blankly.

Vorg smiled reminiscently. 'Surely you've seen it, Doctor? The quickness of the hand deceives the eye? You see, you take three magum pods and a yarrow seed . . .'

'All right, all right,' snapped the Doctor. 'I believe I have seen something similar. So—you won the Scope from a fellow showman and you don't know how it works?'

'Well, I can manage the basic operating procedures,' said Vorg. 'But as for all this technical stuff.' He shook his head sadly.

The Doctor thought for a moment. 'This Wallarian you won the Scope from . . . did he give you a blue or green disc, about this size?' The Doctor formed a circle with finger and thumb.

Vorg stroked his moustache. 'Hard to say. He gave me all sorts of odds and ends. Most of 'em are in my old bag here.' Vorg fished out a well-worn plastic tool-bag, and displayed the contents—an amazing assortment of electronic odds and ends. The Doctor started sorting through them.

'What's your plan, Doctor?' asked Shirna.

The Doctor went on searching as he talked. 'Well, basically it's very simple. The Omega circuit on the Scope is beyond repair. But if I link it to my TARDIS I can use that as the master over-ride and reprogramme the Scope's Space/Time continuum circuitry.'

Shirna hadn't understood a word. 'And what will that do?'

'Two things, I hope. It will expel my friend and myself from inside the Scope. And when the Scope finally does break down it will automatically return the other life-forms inside to their original Space/Time co-ordinates.'

'You mean they'll all go back where they came from?'

'I sincerely hope so,' said the Doctor. 'If my scheme works, they'll arrive at precisely the same point of time in which they left, and never know their lives have been interrupted. But I must have that Omega by-pass disc . . .'

Vorg stuck a hand into the bag and pulled out a grimy disc. 'This what you want? Bit mucky, I'm afraid.'

The Doctor grabbed the disc from him. 'Thank heavens. Now, I'll show you what I want you to do. Wait there a moment, will you?' He ran over to the TARDIS and disappeared inside.

Near by, Kalik and Orum had noticed the vibrating panel at the bottom of the Scope. In his slow-witted way Orum had been pondering Kalik's plan, and had spotted a flaw. 'Is it not possible,' he inquired mildly, 'that when the Drashigs break out of the Scope, one will become oneself involved in the disaster?'

Kalik said impatiently. 'There is a certain minimal risk.'

Orum blinked. 'One has no wish to be devoured by some alien monstrosity, Kalik. Even in the cause of political progress.' He cheered up. 'However, since there seems little sign that the Drashigs actually will escape . . .'

'Does there not?' Kalik pointed to the base panel. The vibration was perceptibly stronger now.

Orum shook his head doubtfully. 'The outer plates appear to be made of molectic bonded disillium. Their strength is formidable.'

'Indeed,' snapped Kalik. 'Then perhaps one should give the Drashigs a little help.'

Kalik and Orum moved away as the Doctor came out of the TARDIS, playing out lengths of cable and clutching a kind of portable switchboard under one arm.

Vorg and Shirna watched him wire the switchboard into the inner workings of the Scope. He straightened up. 'There,' he said.

Vorg looked dubiously at the tangle of wires. 'Is that it? It doesn't look very safe.'

'Oh, you'll be all right if you don't touch any bare metal,' said the Doctor casually. 'Now then, Vorg, I've made it all very simple for you. This is the phase one switch. I'm hoping it will get me into the Scope at a point very close to where my friend is. This is the phase two switch.'

'Phase one switch, phase two switch,' muttered Vorg, hoping he could remember all these technicalities.

The Doctor gave him a despairing look. 'Now concentrate, Vorg, this is very important. I'll need all the time I can get once I'm inside—and the phase two switch is the dematerialiser. So don't pull the phase two switch until the very last minute, when the Scope is about to break down completely. If you pull the switch too early, it just won't work.'

Vorg nodded, scowling in concentration. 'Phase one switch when you tell me, phase two switch at the last minute. Right!'

Pletrac, who had been watching suspiciously for some time, came bustling over to them. 'What is going on here?'

Excitedly Shirna said, 'The Doctor's going back inside the Scope to rescue his friend!'

Pletrac was horrified. 'He will do no such thing.' He addressed the Doctor sternly. 'You have come here illegally. You will be sent to the I.C.C.A. for investigation.'

'What's that?' asked the Doctor. Pletrac had the aggravating suspicion that the alien wasn't really listening to him.

Vorg answered the Doctor's question. 'The I.C.C.A. is the Inner Constellations Corrective Authority. You won't like it, Doctor.'

'In other words it's a prison?'

'One has no wish to be unduly harsh,' said Pletrac. 'But people like you must be taught that rules and regulations are made to be·observed. You are, it appears, something of a vagabond.'

The Doctor grinned. 'Oh yes, very much so,' he admitted cheerfully. Changing his tone he snapped, '*Now* Vorg—phase one!' The Doctor leaned as far inside the Scope's inspection-hatch as he could get.

Vorg gasped stupidly at him for a moment. Then, remembering his instructions and muttering, 'Phase one, phase one,' he leaned over the switchboard and pulled the phase one switch.

The Doctor vanished.

12

The End of the Scope

Pletrac was enraged by this fresh defiance of his authority. 'Stop,' he yelled. 'Come back at once!' What really annoyed him was the fact that the Doctor seemed to have disappeared inside an inspection-hatch which was obviously too small to hold him.

With a flash of childish rage, Pletrac swiped the Doctor's rigged-up switchboard with his blaster. There was a crackle and a flash. Pletrac jumped back, sucking his fingers as the blaster flew from his hand.

Vorg and Shirna ran to the switchboard. The phase two switch was a smoking ruin. Vorg sighed. 'Well, at least he's back inside the Scope all right.'

Shirna said, 'Maybe he is! But how are we going to get him out?'

The Doctor felt a swirling dizziness, then he lost consciousness for a moment as the compression-field of the Scope sucked him in. He recovered quickly, and found himself draped across a broken circuit, fairly close to the tunnel that led back to the ship's hold. As he made his way through the interior of the Scope the Doctor was shocked to see how quickly damage and deterioration had spread. It was clear that the Scope wasn't going to function much longer. He had a strictly limited time in which to find Jo.

Jo had been waiting in the hold for what seemed like ages. She was beginning to fear the Doctor would never come. She sat with her eyes fixed on the octagonal plate in the floor of the hold, willing it to move, but nothing happened. She considered trying to climb through the torn gap left by the Drashig, but the climb looked steep and dangerous. And there was always the horrid possibility of meeting another Drashig on its way up. She wondered how long she could stay down here undetected. It had taken her only minutes to get the cabin door open, and there had been no one about when she'd crossed the deck and climbed down the cargo-hatch. She was hoping that when they did discover she was no longer in the cabin, they would search the rest of the ship before trying the hold again.

Jo's reveries were interrupted by a metallic sliding sound. She leaned forward. The octagonal panel in the floor was moving back, and to her joy the head and shoulders of the Doctor appeared through it. 'Jo?' he called. 'Jo, are you there?'

Sheer relief somehow made Jo irritable. 'Well, of course I'm here! I've been here for ages. Where have you *been*, Doctor?'

'No time for questions,' said the Doctor. 'Come on, we've got to get out of here.'

He led Jo along the same route as before, down the long tube and through the machinery towards the sheer drop. Once they arrived, there was only the long climb down and then they'd be free ... In actual fact, they should be free when Vorg pulled the phase two switch; if the Doctor's plan worked, they ought then to dematerialise outside the Scope. But the Doctor wanted to get Jo out before that if possible, just in case Vorg let him down, or something else went wrong. He had no way of knowing just how badly things had gone wrong already.

Urged on by Shirna, Vorg was doing his not very competent best to repair the phase two switch. He had never been much of a technician, but as Shirna had pointed out, only the switch was really damaged—the rest of the improvised switchboard was unharmed. And surely a switch was a switch. Vorg seemed all thumbs as he worked, but as her technical knowledge was even less than his, Shirna had no alternative than to let him get on with it.

'How's it coming, Vorg?' she asked urgently.

'Not long now,' he grunted. 'Just a few more connections.'

Shirna took a serrated crystal strip from Vorg's bag. 'Is this bit any use?' she asked.

Vorg looked up at the strip and stopped working in amazement. 'I'm sure that wasn't there before,' he said. (Vorg was quite right. Kalik had taken advantage of the confusion caused by the Doctor's disappearance to toss it into the tool-bag.)

Shirna held up the crystal strip. 'What is it then?'

'Focusing Tryzon for an Eradicator gun.' Vorg took the little strip and sighed reminiscently. 'Haven't seen one of these for years. Not since I served in the old 14th Heavy Lasers. Our battery sergeant was a crustacoid mercenary and ...'

'Never mind the military reminiscences,' interrupted Shirna. 'Just you finish repairing that switch. The power's nearly down to critical ...'

Vorg stuffed the strip in his pocket, and got back to work.

They were almost at the top of the shaft when Jo started slowing down. 'Come on, Jo,' urged the Doctor. 'Not much further now ...'

Jo stumbled and fell. 'Sorry, Doctor. Can't seem to get my ... breath ...' Her head fell back.

The Doctor could feel his own strength flagging. It was getting darker and colder as the Scope started to run down, and the air was becoming dangerously thin. The Doctor hoisted Jo on to his shoulders and staggered on.

In the passenger saloon Major Daly looked up from his book. It actually seemed to be cold. Cold in the tropics! And it was getting dark too. A freak tropical storm, perhaps.

Clare ran into the saloon. 'Daddy, what's happening?' she cried. 'I don't feel ...'

Daly struggled out of his chair. It seemed to take a very long time. Andrews staggered in and stood staring down at Clare.

'Give me a hand, old chap,' said Daly reprovingly. 'Poor gel's suffering from heat exhaustion. Should never have brought her ...'

He collapsed, slumping backwards in his chair. Andrews knelt beside Clare and tried to lift her. Then he pitched over sideways, falling across her body.

The three bodies lay motionless, while the little saloon grew colder and darker ...

The Doctor staggered along a metal-walled tunnel, Jo on his back. He knew it was hopeless. Even if he reached the rope, he'd never manage to climb down it, carrying Jo.

As the top of the shaft came in sight, the Doctor slumped to his knees, lowering Jo gently to the ground. 'The phase two switch, Vorg,' he muttered. 'Press the phase two switch.' He slid forwards on to his face ...

All over the Scope life-forms were collapsing. Ogrons, Cybermen, Ice Warriors ... Only the indomitable Drashigs hurled themselves time and time again against the base plates ...

Vorg looked up. 'Right,' he said. 'This is the last connection.'

Kalik and Orum were at the other side of the Scope, watching the vibrating base plate. It was so nearly free now ... They saw Pletrac coming towards them, a Spaceport Functionary at his side. 'Too late, Kalik,' said Orum mournfully. 'Pletrac is here. The Transporter has arrived. There will be no rebellion.'

Kalik could not bear to see his dreams of power snatched away—and all for the want of a few more seconds.

'Orum,' he ordered. 'Go and delay Pletrac. I don't care what you say or do—just delay him!'

Orum was dubious, but obedient as always. 'One will do one's best.'

As Orum moved to intercept Pletrac, Kalik grabbed a crowbar from Vorg's tool-kit, and began prising at the base plate of the Scope. Busily finishing the last switch connection, it took Vorg a moment to notice him. Then, suddenly seeing what Kalik was doing, Vorg rushed round the Scope.

'Stop that,' he yelled. 'Do you want to get us all killed?'

Kalik, his face a fanatical mask, produced his blaster. 'Get back, or you'll be killed now,' he snarled. Covering Vorg with the blaster, he prised away at the Scope one-handed.

Orum was trying to think of reasons to delay Pletrac, but imagination had never been his strong point.

'For the last time, the special Transporter was delayed by a refusal of Engineering Functionaries to work double shifts,' said Pletrac pettishly. 'Now, will you please get out of my way.' He sidestepped past Orum and immediately saw what Kalik was doing— just as Kalik succeeded in prising loose a corner of the base plate.

The Drashig grew so fast it seemed to materialise from thin air. Once at its full terrifying size, its neck swung round, its teeth gnashed. It let out a terrifying bellow at the scent of so much edible flesh in one place. Knocking Orum aside, Pletrac ran to the Eradicator. Seizing the controls he swung it round and fired. Nothing happened. 'Sabotage! Run for your lives,' Pletrac screamed.

The advice was unnecessary. Everyone in the Spaceport was already running.

Kalik sprinted across the Spaceport, the Drashig at his heels, its claws scrabbling on the smooth floor.

Kalik stumbled and rolled over. The Drashig's head swooped down, and Kalik swung wildly with the crowbar. The Drashig ate him, crowbar and all. Its appetite barely whetted, the Drashig swung round in quest of more prey. Shirna stood beside the Scope too terrified to move. The Drashig bore down on her.

Afterwards Vorg could never understand how he managed to move so quickly. He'd watched everything in bemused amazement, Kalik prising off the plate, the Drashig materialising, Pletrac's attempt to use the Eradicator, Kalik's sudden and horrible death ... All at once Vorg realised what he had to do. Grabbing Shirna by the hand, he dragged her across to the Eradicator, thrusting her down behind it for shelter. Jumping into the control seat, he took the Tryzon Focuser from his pocket, slid it into the mechanism, swung round the Eradicator nozzle and fired ...

By now the Drashig was almost upon him and the full blast of the Eradicator beam took it straight between the slavering jaws. The Drashig bellowed, glowed bright red, then disappeared, completely disintegrated by the Eradicator beam.

There was another fearsome bellow, and Vorg saw a second Drashig bearing down upon him. With calm professionalism, Vorg swung the Eradicator on to the new target and pressed the firing button ...

One by one the Drashigs came from the machine, shooting up to full size. One by one Vorg blasted them into nothingness. When the last monster was disposed of, Vorg stepped down from the gun, dusting his hands together. 'Well,' he said casually. 'That's that!'

Shirna straightened up, looking at this new heroic Vorg with unbelieving eyes. Suddenly she shouted,

'Don't stand there preening yourself, Vorg! What about the Doctor?'

They ran across to the Scope. Vorg looked at the dials all flickering on their lowest readings. 'It's too late,' he said sadly. 'I finished repairing the switch, but there's no power to work it.'

'At least we can try,' said Shirna.

Vorg threw the switch. 'It's no use—the power's completely gone ...' He paused, listening. 'No, wait a minute ...'

A faint hum of power was coming through the Doctor's keyboard. It grew in strength as the failing Scope was able to draw power from the TARDIS console. Slowly the power-hum began to build, till the Scope was vibrating with energy.

In the misty swamp, a Drashig raised its head, bellowed—and vanished.

The prostrate bodies of Major Daly, his daughter Clare and young Lieutenant Andrews faded quietly away from the saloon of the S.S. *Bernice*.

All over the Scope, in all the different circuits, Ogrons, Cybermen, Ice Warriors and a variety of other life-forms faded away, to reappear back on their original planets.

Deep inside the machinery of the Scope, the bodies of Jo and the Doctor dematerialised ...

. . . to appear in the Spaceport of Inter Minor, sprawled at the base of the TARDIS, just as the Doctor had planned. They recovered consciousness to find a delighted Vorg and Shirna standing over them. Helped by the two Lurmans, Jo and the Doctor got to their feet. Vorg shook the Doctor enthusiastically by the hand. 'It worked, Doctor, it worked,' he shouted.

The Doctor grinned. 'So I see. You cut it a bit fine, didn't you?'

Vorg gave a modest smile. 'As a matter of fact, Doctor, we had a little trouble here—but I dealt with it.'

Jo recovered to find the Doctor and a lot of oddly-dressed strangers smiling down at her. The Doctor lifted her to her feet. 'It's all right, Jo, we made it!' He pointed to the TARDIS just behind them.

Jo gave a sigh of relief. 'What about all the others though?' she asked. 'The people on the ship?'

The Doctor was putting on his coat. 'They're all right too,' he said. 'I reversed the Scope's original settings and linked them to the TARDIS. They should all be back on their ship.'

'The real ship this time? The real S.S. *Bernice*, sailing the real Indian Ocean, back in the year nineteen twenty-six?'

The Doctor nodded. 'Exactly!'

Jo smiled. 'I'm glad about that. I grew quite fond of them all in the end. Won't that mean changing history though?'

The Doctor waved his hand airily. 'Only in a few very small details.'

Propped up in his bunk, Major Daly finished the last

page of his book. There was a tap on the cabin door, and his daughter Clare came in. 'It's only me. I've come to say good night.'

Daly yawned. 'I've been reading,' he said sleepily. 'Actually managed to finish my book. Seems like the longest one I ever read.'

Clare nodded, gazing through the porthole at the setting sun. 'It does seem to have been a long trip somehow . . .'

Daly tapped his book. 'Disappointing ending. Chap decided to become a missionary. Thought he'd marry the girl.'

Clare smiled. 'You're an old romantic, Daddy. I'll bet all your stories about the East are just romances.'

'See for yourself, soon. Bombay tomorrow.'

Clare stood up. 'I'm really looking forward to that.'

Daly smiled slyly. 'Not sure young Andrews is—he wouldn't care how long this trip lasted.'

Clare laughed. 'That's what I mean. You're a romantic! Good night, Daddy.' She kissed his cheek and went out of the cabin.

Daly yawned again. He reached out for his calendar and crossed off the last day of the voyage, then settled down to sleep. As he was drifting off, strange pictures floated through his mind. He heard the roar of guns, and the bellowing of monsters. There was something about a tall white-haired man, and a small girl with fair hair . . . stowaways . . . Daly couldn't make any sense of it. Must be jumbled memories of some blood and thunder story he'd read a long time ago. Soon he was peacefully asleep. The S.S. *Bernice* steamed steadily towards Bombay.

Surrounded by an admiring audience of Officials and Functionaries, Vorg was telling the story of his valour for the hundreth time. '... then came the second Drashig, barrelling-in at ninety degrees. It was so close I could feel its breath. So I swung like this, see, and gave it a quick burst. Then the third—I got that one with a snap shot ...'

'Indeed we are all very grateful,' interrupted Pletrac politely. 'Your valour will long be remembered.'

'It will if he has anything to do with it,' muttered Shirna.

'Think nothing of it,' Vorg was saying. 'As an old soldier it's my natural reaction to stand and fight ... Well, as I was saying ...'

The Doctor tapped Pletrac gently on the shoulder. 'I think it's time we were leaving.'

Pletrac was horrified. 'Out of the question. You must all stay for the Court of Inquiry. Orum has confessed. He and Kalik plotted to discredit our President. They sabotaged the Eradicator and aided the Drashigs to escape.'

'Well, there you are then,' said Jo. 'If you've got a confession you don't need an Inquiry.'

'One must observe the correct procedures,' said Pletrac.

The Doctor gave Jo a warning nudge. 'They're very hot on correct procedures here, Jo. Better not argue— it's a waste of time.'

Pletrac gave a satisfied nod. At last the alien was learning correct behaviour. Jo gave the Doctor an understanding smile. They started edging towards the TARDIS.

Pletrac turned his attention back to Vorg. 'President

Zarb will no doubt wish to reward your valour with some appropriate decoration.'

'A medal,' said Vorg happily. 'How very kind.'

Shirna nudged him. 'We can't eat medals, Vorg. How are we going to live now the Scope's just a heap of old junk?'

Vorg gave a confident smile. 'Just you leave that to me, my dear.'

As the Doctor opened the TARDIS door, Vorg was turning to Pletrac.

'Now then, old fellow, I'm going to show you a little game.'

Pletrac gave him a puzzled look. 'What is a game?'

Vorg was arranging three polished pods on the top of a crate. They were circular and hollow, like little wooden cups. He turned them upside down and produced a bright blue seed, holding it up between finger and thumb.

'Now, you see these three magum pods? I'm going to put this yarrow seed under the middle one, right?'

Pletrac nodded, completely baffled.

'Then,' said Vorg in a hypnotic voice, 'I move the magum pods about very slowly, like so ... Now, which one is the seed under?'

'There is no possible doubt,' said Pletrac unhesitatingly. 'This one!'

'Quite right,' said Vorg encouragingly, lifting up the pod. 'Now then, care to try again? How about a little wager, just to add interest?'

He replaced the seed, and moved the pods about.

'Very well,' said Pletrac obligingly. 'We will wager one credit-bar. The seed is under—this one!' He was wrong.

124

Pletrac was indignant. 'We shall play again,' he insisted. 'One was too hasty. One will not be mistaken a second time.'

'Another small wager,' suggested Vorg casually. 'Increase the stake a bit?'

Pletrac frowned. It was intolerable that he, a senior Official of Inter Minor, should be bested in such a simple game. 'Most certainly,' he said. 'One will wager five—no ten credit-bars that one's judgement is correct.'

Vorg beamed and winked at Shirna. 'I think I'm going to like it here, Pletrac old fellow. I can see you Minorans are great sportsmen. You remind me of the Wallarians . . .'

Jo had been watching in fascination. The Doctor tapped her on the shoulder. 'Time to be off, Jo.'

She smiled. 'No need to worry about Vorg, is there? He'll probably end up President!'

'That or Chancellor of the Exchequer,' agreed the Doctor.

They slipped inside the TARDIS.

It caused another mild panic when the TARDIS dematerialised. Officials and Functionaries jumped back in alarm. Shirna smiled rather tearfully, and waved good-bye.

Commissioner Pletrac didn't even notice. He was trying to work out how he'd managed to pick the wrong magum pod yet again . . .

DOCTOR WHO

0426101103	DAVID WHITAKER **Doctor Who and The** **Daleks**	£1.50
042611244X	TERRANCE DICKS **Doctor Who and The Dalek** **Invasion of Earth**	£1.50
0426103807	**Doctor Who and The Day** **of the Daleks**	£1.35
042620042X	**Doctor Who – Death to** **the Daleks**	£1.35
0426119657	**Doctor Who and The** **Deadly Assassin**	£1.50
0426200969	**Doctor Who and The** **Destiny of the Daleks**	£1.35
0426108744	MALCOLM HULKE **Doctor Who and The** **Dinosaur Invasion**	£1.35
0426103726	**Doctor Who and** **The Doomsday Weapon**	£1.50
0426201464	IAN MARTER **Doctor Who and The** **Enemy of the World**	£1.50
0426200063	TERRANCE DICKS **Doctor Who and The** **Face of Evil**	£1.50
0426201507	ANDREW SMITH **Doctor Who – Full Circle**	£1.50
0426112601	TERRANCE DICKS **Doctor Who and The** **Genesis of the Daleks**	£1.35
0426112792	**Doctor Who and The Giant Robot**	£1.35
0426115430	MALCOLM HULKE **Doctor Who and The** **Green Death**	£1.35

Prices are subject to alteration

DOCTOR WHO

0426200330	TERRANCE DICKS **Doctor Who and The** **Hand of Fear**	£1.35
0426201310	**Doctor Who and The** **Horns of Nimon**	£1.35
0426200098	**Doctor Who and The** **Horror of Fang Rock**	£1.35
0426108663	BRIAN HAYLES **Doctor Who and The** **Ice Warriors**	£1.35
0426200772	**Doctor Who and The** **Image of the Fendahl**	£1.35
0426200934	TERRANCE DICKS **Doctor Who and The** **Invasion of Time**	£1.35
0426200543	**Doctor Who and The** **Invisible Enemy**	£1.35
0426201485	**Doctor Who and The** **Keeper of Traken**	£1.35
0426201256	PHILIP HINCHCLIFFE **Doctor Who and The** **Keys of Marinus**	£1.35
0426201477	DAVID FISHER **Doctor Who and The** **Leisure Hive**	£1.35
0426110412	TERRANCE DICKS **Doctor Who and The** **Loch Ness Monster**	£1.25
0426201493	CHRISTOPHER H BIDMEAD **Doctor Who – Logopolis**	£1.35
0426118936	PHILIP HINCHCLIFFE **Doctor Who and The** **Masque of Mandragora**	£1.25
0426201329	TERRANCE DICKS **Doctor Who and The** **Monster of Peladon**	£1.35

Prices are subject to alteration

STAR Books are obtainable from many booksellers and newsagents. If you have any difficulty please send purchase price plus postage on the scale below to:

> **Star Cash Sales**
> **P.O. Box 11**
> **Falmouth**
> **Cornwall**
> OR
> **Star Book Service,**
> **G.P.O. Box 29,**
> **Douglas,**
> **Isle of Man,**
> **British Isles.**

While every effort is made to keep prices low, it is sometimes necessary to increase prices at short notice. Star Books reserve the right to show new retail prices on covers which may differ from those advertised in the text or elsewhere.

Postage and Packing Rate
UK: 55p for the first book, 22p for the second book and 14p for each additional book ordered to a maximum charge of £1.75p. BFPO and EIRE: 55p for the first book, 22p for the second book, 14p per copy for the next 7 books, thereafter 8p per book. Overseas: £1.00p for the first book and 25p per copy for each additional book.